THRILLER, HORROR, MYSTERY, COZY...AND MORE

2026 ANTHOLOGY

A COLLECTION OF SHORT STORIES PENNED BY MEMBERS OF SLEUTHS' INK.

CONTRIBUTORS

Jen Kenning – Gil Miller – Tim Ritter – Ana Hurst
Margarite Stever – Art William L. Breach
Shirley McCann – David C. Reed
J.C. Fields – R.H. Burkett – Susan Keene
Clarissa Willis – Lois Curran – M.E. Rowe
Sharon Kizziah-Holmes – J.C. Crumpton – Lynn Combs

Book & Cover Design – Sharon Kizziah-Holmes

Paperback-Press
an imprint of Paperback Press, LLC
Springfield, Missouri

ISBN -13: 978-1-970560-13-8

Dedication

To the members of
Sleuths' Ink Mystery Writers current and past.

TABLE OF CONTENTS – BY AUTHOR

Acknowledgments

Thank you, Venessa Cerasale, for your editing expertise. We appreciate the time you put in on each story.

Shirley McCann and Lois Curran, your proofreading of the final draft is priceless.

Sharon Kizziah-Holmes, thank you and Paperback Press for your cover and interior book design. You are valued.

Jen Kenning

Jen's worked as a maid, waitress, cook, horseback riding trail guide, insurance adjuster, fire & theft investigator, customer service tech, and reference librarian. Her favorite jobs were trail guide and librarian. She holds a Bachelor's of Science degree in Criminal Justice and Psychology and an Associate of Science in Paralegal Studies. She currently lives on a family farm with her son and a bunch of creatures. When she's not writing she's growing food and making jewelry.

A Note to Readers:

Thank you so much for reading my work, I truly hope you enjoy it! If you'd like to keep up with what I'm working on, please check out my website jenkenningauthor.com or follow me on Facebook.

On the website you'll find recipes, blog articles, and a newsletter signup (totally optional). Eventually some short stories will make an appearance there.

Leaving reviews and/or stars is a great way to support my writing and it's free to do.

Another Shot

Tom leaned back in his recliner. His bowl of popcorn on the side table, and the TV tuned for Monday Night Football. He popped the cap off his beer and took a deep swig. He'd been in a rut since the divorce and football season was the only thing he looked forward to.

Kickoff was imminent. Tom's cell phone sounded the ringtone assigned to his work. The theme song from Hawaii Five-0 blared at him.

"Dammit." He leaned forward and grabbed the phone off the coffee table. "Hello, whatcha got?"

The voice on the other end of the phone was Sergeant Roger Adkins. Never one to bother with extra words, pleasant or otherwise, he said, "Adkins here. We got a body behind the bar on 5th street. Meat wagon is on the way. Go."

Tom was already moving. He regretted opening the beer. He wasn't impaired, and it would be stale when he got home. He grabbed his badge and holstered service weapon on his way out the door.

The Kojak light on his older model Crown Vic swirled and he flipped the toggle to turn on the siren.

Applejack, Oklahoma had a small geographical footprint. It was home to around 4800 people. There were only two bars. One on 5th street and the other was close to the square on Main. Tom was familiar with both.

Tom's gut twisted when he wondered who was dead

behind the bar. The bar his ex-wife's uncle owned. The bar Evelyn had worked at ever since they met and subsequently married seven years ago. He floored the accelerator.

He slid to a stop in the parking lot of the bar. Dust boiled up from the chat driveway. It hadn't rained in weeks. There was a patrol car parked on the left side of the lot with lights flashing but no siren. Tom walked over and contacted Officer Perez.

"Hey Cheryl, what do we know so far?"

Officer Cheryl Perez looked up from her task of stringing yellow crime scene tape across the back door of the building. "Hi, Tom, I'm glad to see you. I'm spread a little thin here by myself." She pointed to the dumpster. "The deceased is in there. From what I can see, the victim is Caucasian male and hasn't been there very long."

Tom sighed and peeked over the side of the dumpster. He agreed with Perez's assessment. "Who found the body?"

Perez snorted. "You're going to hate this. It was Evelyn. She's inside waiting to give her statement."

"Terrific." Tom hung his head, turned on his heel and headed for the front door of Charlie's Pub.

The bar was dimly lit, cool and not nearly as smoky as one might expect. Tom removed his sunglasses and made a mental note of the number and type of patrons inside the building.

He noticed an older couple in a corner booth. They had a couple of beers and a basket of fries between them. Two twenty somethings were shooting pool. He scanned them for potential risks. His gut told him they were okay, at least for now.

Evelyn was behind the bar. She had the cordless phone cradled in the crook of her neck, and she was wiping water spots from a glass with a towel. She hung up the phone.

Tom noticed she'd changed her hair. It was shorter and had streaks in it. He watched her register his arrival. He never could tell what she was thinking based on her expression. *Some detective I am. That's probably one of the reasons we split.*

Evelyn put the glass on the rack and tossed the towel on the counter. "Tom. Fancy seeing you here. Of course it would be you, you're the only damn detective in the county."

The perceived bitterness in her words stung him. He forced a smile. "That makes me the best man for the job then. You found the body, right? Tell me about it." He opened his notebook and patted his pocket in search of his pen.

Evelyn smirked and slid a ballpoint pen across the bar. "You never could keep track of your pen. There's not much to tell. I came on shift at three p.m. The place was a mess because we're short-handed. I spent the first couple hours cleaning. By the time I collected the trash from the washrooms, the big cans were full. I took them out. When I lifted the dumpster lid to toss in the bags, I saw the dead guy. I called the station and then I threw up."

Tom resisted the urge to walk behind the bar and wrap his ex in a hug. "I'm sorry you went through that. You look pale, do you still feel queasy?"

"Yes, but I'll be okay."

"Did you recognize the deceased?"

"No, I didn't see his face. It all kinda blurred together. The thing that stood out was the arrows sticking out of him."

Tom's stomach clenched. "Arrows are a bit unusual for a murder weapon. Given your archery expertise, I'd like to hear your thoughts."

Evelyn cocked her head and put her hand on her hip. "Is that a thinly veiled dig, or maybe it's an accusation?"

His voice ratcheted up. "It's neither one. Evie, you won awards for archery in high school. You could've gotten a scholarship if you'd wanted. I'm asking for your opinion on the arrows. Getting so damn defensive for no apparent reason makes you look guilty, though."

They both noticed the other patrons watching them.

Evie leaned forward and whispered, "Lower your voice. You don't get to yell at me anymore. I don't know a damn thing about those arrows, except they aren't mine."

Tom took a deep breath and let it out slowly. "I'm not yelling. We'll need a list of all the people that were here today. Employees and patrons. If you don't know the patrons' names, please provide what you can in the way of physical descriptions, credit card numbers, or known associates. I'll follow up with you tomorrow. Where's your Uncle Charlie?"

"He's not here. I don't know where he is. I called and left a message on his answering machine. He's old school, doesn't keep a cell phone."

"Yeah. I know. He's a dinosaur, but I always liked him. Give me his number and if you talk to him first, please tell him to call me." Tom pocketed the napkin with Charlie's phone number and made a mental note not to wash it.

Tom spoke to the other occupants of the bar and gathered their names, numbers, and jotted down the times each arrived at the pub. He returned to the parking lot. The coroner's van was positioned near the scene. He realized they were waiting on him.

Tom noted Perez was flipping through photos on a digital camera. He walked over and asked, "Do you have the pics we need? I'll tell them to transport the body."

"Yes, I've got every angle. You're welcome to check the photos." She extended the camera toward him.

He waved it off. "I trust ya. Did you look outside the dumpster for tire tracks and footprints?"

"I did, and I took photos even though nothing stood out.

The gravel is so dry it would take something heavy to leave a good print. I did find a clump of chewing tobacco. It looked fresh so I bagged it. It was gross."

Perez shrugged. "There's not much here. Maybe they'll find some prints or something with the arrows. Weird choice for a murder weapon. Poor guy looks like a pin cushion."

Tom gave a thumbs up sign to the medical personnel. They began to retrieve the body for transport. He walked over to speak with the coroner. "Hey Paul, can you remove the arrows tonight? I suspect they stick out too far to fit in the cold drawer. I've got to collect them and get them to the crime lab. Chain of evidence and all that."

"Yeah, we can do that. I figured as much."

The county coroner operated out of the basement of Paul Davis and Sons Mortuary. Paul Davis had functioned as the coroner for over twenty years.

The basement was kept very cold. It was well lit and exceptionally clean.

Tom shivered and mentally steeled himself against the sights, sounds, and smells as Paul began to remove the arrows.

The coroner placed the arrows in a plastic-lined box for transport. The process was photographed, and the box was labeled. The victim's clothing was bagged and tagged as well.

"Here ya go, Tom. I hope you find some useful clues. I'll have a full report for you in a few days, but I should have preliminary cause of death tomorrow."

"Thank you, Paul."

Tom tucked the box of evidence under his arm and trudged back to his car. Twenty minutes later he walked into the police department.

The forensic technicians from the Oklahoma State Bureau of Investigation were waiting for him. They stood and exchanged greetings.

Tom placed the box of evidence on the desk. “It’s good to see both of you again. Did you find anything useful at the scene?”

Rob shook his head. “We bagged the dumpster contents. We’ll go through them at the shop. Better lighting, no wind blowing stuff around.”

Sally sipped her coffee. “We took possession of the chewing tobacco collected by Officer Perez. We’ll start processing all of it first thing in the morning.”

By noon the next day, Tom had identified the victim as 47-year-old Darren Graft. Mr. Graft was known to law enforcement in his hometown, Tulsa, for petty theft and domestic abuse. His chosen vocation was dealing drugs.

Tom skimmed his emails. Two were of interest. The autopsy revealed that arrows pierced the victim’s liver and lung. A third arrow sliced the femoral artery and Graft bled out.

The other email came from Sally. She’d found a broken fingernail among the victim’s clothes. It had red polish on it as well as blood. Tom studied the attached photo. His cell pinged with a text from Evelyn. It said, *need you at the bar now.*

Tom walked into the pub, removed his sunglasses, and read the room. The early afternoon crowd was sparse.

Evie came from behind the bar and grabbed Tom’s arm.

"Charlie's back and has a tale to tell you. He's pretty shook up, so be nice."

"I'm always nice. Where is he?"

"In the back. Come on."

Evie led Tom through the swinging door behind the bar. Her elderly uncle sat at a small table.

Tom took the chair across from the man. He noticed Charlie's hand shook when he picked up his drink. "Hey Charlie, what's up?"

Charlie sipped his beer. "I found something out at the farm. I think it's where the guy died. I think I might be next."

Tom leaned forward. "Tell me everything."

Charlie met Tom's eyes. "I stayed home yesterday with the flu. This morning, I walked out to the south field to find my dog. She hadn't come back like usual. I found her guarding a patch of grass that was covered in blood. There was no body. I took Kelso back to the house. When I got into my truck to leave for the bar I found a bloody note on my windshield."

The old man removed a crumpled note from his pocket and pushed it across the table to Tom.

"Your days servin' minors are 'bout over." Charlie winced when Tom read it aloud. "Tom, I swear I've never knowingly served minors. We check IDs. The fakes get better every year."

Tom fished an evidence bag from his pocket and placed the note inside. "I believe you. I'm sending a team out to process the scene where you found the blood. Can you think who would have a grudge against you? Did you know the victim?" He'd laid a photo of Graft on the table.

Charlie peered at the photo and shook his head. "I don't know him. Can't swear he'd never been in the bar, though."

A scream out in the bar got both men on their feet. A shot rang out. Tom motioned for Charlie to get behind him. He crept to the door and eased it open an inch. He saw a middle-aged blonde with a small caliber gun in hand. Evie was huddled behind the bar. The other patrons had scattered.

The woman stood in the middle of the dining area, blocking the door. Her face was a mess of tears, snot, and mascara. She pointed the gun at the kitchen door, and her hand shook. "Old man, get out here. You're the last on my list. I can end this and be with my baby girl on the other side."

Tom checked Charlie to see if he knew what this was about. A negative head shake was the response. He eased the door open further. "Ma'am, I'm an officer of the law. I want to help you. Tell me how to help you."

Blondie fired a round at the kitchen door. "The hell you do. Where were you when my baby overdosed on drugs and alcohol? It's taken me fifteen years to track down the dealer and lure him back here. My girl would have turned twenty-nine yesterday. She died behind this miserable bar. Drowned in her own vomit."

Tom chanced a look out the door at Evie. He saw her crouched behind the bar, scribbling on her order book. She ripped a page off, crumpled it up and tossed it toward Tom. He bent low and retrieved the tiny paper.

15 years ago, Amanda Barclay died of drug od and alcohol poisoning in the ally. Think this is her mom, Karen. She was on the archery team.

Tom stood. "Karen, I'm so sorry about your daughter. I remember that case. Put your gun down and talk to me."

"You're sorry all right. Gonna give me 'thoughts and prayers next?" Karen emptied her gun into bottles of liquor behind the bar. She crumpled to floor. Her body racked with sobs.

Tom emerged from the kitchen, hurried to Karen and took her gun.

Officer Perez arrived and took Karen into custody.

Evie and Charlie closed the bar. Cleanup could wait.

Tom tapped Evie on the shoulder. When she faced him, he took the broom she held and set it aside. He took her hands in his. "Evelyn, tonight I was terrified to lose you. I know you're mad at me. I want to fix it. We make a good team. If you hadn't remembered who she was, this night may have ended worse. Will you give us another try?"

Evie gazed into his eyes. She cocked her head and smiled a wicked smile. "You big dummy. Yeah, we make a good team. I was scared of losing you tonight too. I think it's worth another shot."

Cloud of Deceit

The blinding glare from the oncoming headlights hurt Tom's eyes. The resultant headache and the empty feeling in his stomach made him grumpy. He'd been driving for hours. The enigmatic note left under his windshield wiper left him jittery. Equal parts excited anticipation and suspicious dread churned within him.

Travel west for five hundred miles. There you will find your treasure. There you will find yourself. Your love and your destiny.

"WTH does that even mean?" Tom muttered. He rubbed his eyes. The digital clock on his dashboard read 2:37 a.m. The trip odometer showed he'd traveled 348 miles.

He yawned and turned up the radio. The next song that came on triggered a mix of good and bad nostalgia. His breath caught and he gripped the steering wheel tighter. She'd swept into his life like a beautiful hurricane. Once his life was upside down, she flitted away to parts unknown. All he knew was that she was gone.

Tom reached for the radio knob and clicked it off. His inner critic chewed on all the things he might have done wrong. Could have done differently. Maybe she would have stayed.

A flash of movement on the left side of the road startled him. A coyote darted into the road. Tom slammed on the brakes and swerved to the right. The creature stopped, caught in the headlights, and it dropped something light colored. The coyote stared at Tom and then took off.

Tom ran his hand through his shoulder length hair. "Holy crap, that was a close one. What is that?" He was grateful the road was deserted. After he double checked both directions for lights, Tom opened the car door and stood up. His ample muscles were stiff and the opportunity to stretch was sweet.

The small cream-colored thing lay where the coyote dropped it. It began to move. Then it whined.

Tom walked over to it and bent down. "Well damn, little dude. You're having a rough night." He scooped up the small creature. Tom identified the wee thing as a puppy of indeterminate breed. "I don't think you're a coyote. Too small to be away from your momma. Guess you're coming with me for now." He scratched the little pup under its chin.

After he settled the puppy on an old sweatshirt on the passenger side floorboard, Tom continued his journey. He saw a sign announcing the next sizable town was twelve miles. Tom decided to find food and stop for a few hours. He could hear the puppy's intermittent whimpers. *Must be hungry. Hope there's an all-night truck stop or big box store up here. Maybe I can find some nice waitress to take the dog off my hands.*

Tom exited the highway and followed the signs for the local Walmart. He parked and went inside. He'd tucked the wee dog in the pocket of his hoodie.

The pet food aisle had some canned milk replacer and two sizes of small bottles. He labored over the decision. One appeared too small and the other may be too large. He bought them both. Tom raided the case near the deli for a couple sub sandwiches and grabbed some chips. He'd brought enough water and a jug of tea.

The puppy whined and wiggled inside his pocket. The young cashier eyed Tom with suspicion but didn't ask any questions.

Once they were back in the car, Tom popped the lid on the canned milk and poured some in the bottle. "Okay little dude, room temperature is as good as it gets. Hope you can cope." He gently stuck the bottle in the tiny maw. After a few minutes of fumbling around, the pup latched on and began to drink.

Tom judged the dog to be full when it let the empty bottle go and belched. Tom laughed. "I think you may be my Spirit Animal." He tucked the little critter into the makeshift bed and wiped his hands on his jeans. Then he dove into his own food. The foot-long sub and the chips assuaged most of his hunger. Tom burped and leaned his seat back. A few hours of shuteye wouldn't hurt.

Bright sunlight streamed through the windows of the car. The comfortable cool nighttime temperature rose rapidly. Tom rubbed his face and peered around. The puppy whined. All the normal human needs combined with the whimpering dog smacked Tom in the head.

"Dang, it got hot fast. I gotta pee. I bet you're hungry again, huh?" Tom tried to wiggle out of his hoodie, but it was too tight in the car. He flung open the door and got out. He couldn't recall the name of the town, so he Googled "breakfast near me". He flopped into the driver's seat and read the list of choices. It was slim. Tom decided to settle for fast food and plotted a course for the closest place.

He ran in and used the men's room. Tom returned to the car and fed his tiny companion a bottle, then he went through the drive-thru for his much-needed coffee and a few breakfast sandwiches. He parked under a shade tree and ate. Tom puzzled over what to do with the little beast. Should he keep it? He'd always liked dogs but didn't think of himself as a dog person. His mind returned to the note. He sighed. *We really need to get on the road. 'We'. Hrumpf. Guess that's my answer.*

Tom drove to the nearest gas station and topped off his tank. His little friend was sound asleep. He drove west until the meter read 500 miles. He was on a minor road in remote Kansas. He pulled into a rest area and wondered what kind of a fool's errand he was on. Who had written the note and what was their end game? Tom sat on the hood of his car and swung his feet. He felt foolish. There had been a tiny hope that she'd left the note, and they would reunite at the conclusion of his journey.

He retrieved the pup from the car and walked toward the visitor center kiosk. It was unmanned but had the normal rack of brochures regarding area attractions. One of the brochures caught his eye. It depicted a bench on a scenic overlook. The words, "Wyatt Wendelin Memorial Bench," were printed in large yellow letters. "Wyatt" was her last name.

Tom picked up the document and flipped it open. Several pictures of the scenery, and a list of other area attractions, adorned the tri-fold paper. One of the pictures showed a coyote poised to howl near the lake bank.

A few mental trinkets clinked around in his head. Never a huge fan of coincidences, Tom searched for reasonable explanations for the odd occurrences. He studied the dog, his surroundings, and the paper he held. "Oh, what the heck? We've come this far. Let's go have a look."

Tom drove to the scenic area and hiked over to the bench. The view was nice. The only sounds were bird song and bull frogs. He sat down and waited for nothing to happen.

He was about to leave when he heard a strange noise. The buzz grew louder. Tom looked all around and saw nothing. Then he looked up. A small drone hovered about ten feet above his head. The machine had been equipped with grippers and held a note in one of them.

Tom watched in awe as the gripper opened and a note wafted down toward him. He snatched it out of midair. He unfolded the note. It brought back memories of middle and high school when passing notes was common. The drone zoomed away.

"Hi Tom, I wondered if you'd come. Hoped you would. Wait a little longer and I'll explain everything. I missed you. x o Mandy."

Tom read the note again and looked in every direction. There wasn't anyone in sight. The puppy wiggled and grunted. *Is this a joke? Is it really from Mandy? Is she coming here?*

So, Tom waited. He waited for over two hours. He began to question the wisdom of continuing to wait. His grief over the lost relationship and the hope of a reunion with the girl of his dreams became overshadowed by feelings of resentment and betrayal. He paced around the bench. It was too hot to sit in the car for long. There was no shade.

He'd fixed a bottle for the little pup and sat on the bench to feed it. Watching the small creature drink was relaxing. Tom marveled at how the tiny creature trusted him entirely. He'd made up his mind to leave.

Tom walked the short distance to his car and saw a vehicle coming down the road toward him. As it got closer, he saw it was a white limo. *What an odd place to see that.* The huge car pulled in beside Tom's car and parked.

The rear door opened, and a young woman got out. She wore a sundress with a jacket and strappy sandals. Her hair was perfectly arranged in an updo, and ringlets of multi-toned blonde hair framed her face. The woman shrieked, "Tom! OMG you waited. How wonderful to see you."

Tom was shocked. This wasn't the girl he met and had a seven-day whirlwind romance with. She'd been down to earth. This lady was beautiful and her face matched Mandy, but some things were vastly different. He raised his eyebrows and cocked his head. "Mandy? Is that really you? What is all this about?"

Mandy sauntered up to Tom and took his hands in hers. She deposited air kisses on both his cheeks. "Of course it's me, who else would it be? I'm so glad you made the trip."

Tom nodded. "Why was the trip necessary? Why did you leave without a word and then weeks later I get a cryptic note on my car? Then I get here and have to wait for almost three hours in the heat. What's the deal? Who are you really?"

Mandy sighed. It was an entitled, put upon type of sigh. "My name is Amanda Marie Garner-Tisdale. My daddy is Hank Tisdale. He told me that I could have any man I want as long as they pass the test. Otherwise, they'd be after our money. So, I figured if a guy genuinely liked me, they'd put forth some effort. Yay! You won!"

Tom ran his hand through his hair and down his face. "Let me make sure I understand. You pretended to be 'Mandy Wyatt the waitress, working her way through college when, in fact, you are an heiress. The mysterious note on my car, the journey into the unknown, keeping me waiting in the heat for hours....was all a test? How did you know where to send the drone?"

"That was easy. I put a tracker on your car under the passenger seat. Neat huh?"

Tom took a deep breath and looked down at the puppy he held. He considered his options.

"What's with the dog? You didn't have it before." Mandy's face was scrunched into a disapproving glower.

Tom gazed at Mandy, her limo and the surrounding area. "I'll be going now. The puppy is the silver lining in this cloud of deceit. Goodbye Mandy or whoever you are."

Tom got into his car and started the engine. He felt around under the seat until he found the tracker. He rolled down his window and chucked the electronic device out. It landed in the dust at Mandy's feet. Tom slammed the car into reverse and spun around. He bit his lip and drove rapidly away before he could change his mind.

Mandy gaped at the retreating car. She waved her hand to fan the dust away.

Tom glanced in his rearview mirror. He saw her standing there. His heart hurt but his gut told him he'd made a good decision. He stroked the soft fur on the puppy's neck. "Your name is Silver. What do you think of that?"

The Black Widow Blues

Darla emerged from the shower in a towel and screamed. “Gary! What the hell are you doing in here? You know the bathroom is off limits.”

Gary slapped his ghostly white hand over his eyes. He bobbed up and down and pointed at Darla’s pile of clothes with his other hand.

“Yeah, yeah. I plan on getting dressed as soon as you get out of here.”

Gary shook his head. A single word appeared on the steamy mirror. “Spider.” He vanished through the closed door. Gary was a ghost.

Darla picked through the articles of clothing. She shook each piece over the sink. A large black spider tumbled out of her folded T-shirt. It had a red mark on its back. An egg sack was stuck to the shirt. “Eww!”

She dropped the shirt in the sink on top of the spider. *Great*. She searched the rest of her clothes and got dressed.

The next several minutes involved finding a different spider-free T-shirt, and scooping Ms. Spider and her egg sack up into a plastic cup. “Looky here, Ms. Spidey. I don’t begrudge you a place to live, but it best not be in my house and ’specially not in my clothes.”

Darla carried the cup to the edge of her property and emptied it gently on an old log. Ever since she’d been attacked and died briefly, she’d been unable to willingly kill anything. Anything except a cockroach. They were entirely too icky to take pity on.

The same event that turned her into an extreme pacifist also left her with the ability to see ghosts. Although the ghosts could hear Darla, she could not hear them. Most of the time she was grateful for this. There were times, like this morning, that a shouted warning from her resident ghost, Gary, would've been preferable to wild hand gestures and words scrawled on a steamed mirror.

"Thanks, Gary! I'm sorry I yelled at you."

The lights flickered twice.

The spider drama used up the few minutes reserved for breakfast, so she grabbed her keys and raced out the door.

The drive-through lane at Brew In A Bucket was long. Darla parked and ran inside. She paid for three large coffees and a baker's dozen of mixed pastries. She arrived at the car to find ghost Gary in the passenger seat. "Hey, Gary, what's shakin'? You rarely leave the house."

When ghosts shrug, it looks more like a ripple.

Darla placed the food in the rear seat. It would be rude to reach through Gary.

Traffic was more beastly than usual. The lane Darla was stuck in hadn't moved for several minutes. She almost regretted the stop at the coffee shop. "The good thing about being the boss is she can make her own schedule. The bad thing is nothing much happens until she gets there."

Gary nodded. Then he pointed at a box truck in the adjacent lane. He kept pointing until Darla looked over at it.

"What? It's a truck. Huh, it's got a spider on it. Weird. So are spiders your exciting new obsession?"

Gary adopted a disgusted expression and vanished.

Darla parked behind her photography studio. It was in a brick building. The cornerstone read 1893. The space had been many things over the years, including a vacant, rat-infested dump. A few years ago, a group of local artists formed a co-op, and with the help of an anonymous benefactor, the building was renovated.

Megan, Darla's assistant, pulled in, parked, and exited her car. "G'morning, Darla. Looks like we're both running a little late."

"Yes, it started out bumpy. I brought coffee and pastries."

"Things are looking up already."

The women entered the studio. Sunlight shown through the front window of the shop. It glistened off a spider web. Darla's jaw dropped open when she saw the web was inhabited by another black spider. She reached to remove it.

Megan grabbed her arm. "Be careful, Darla. That's a black widow spider. They are venomous."

"It's the second one I've encountered today. Third, if you count the truck."

Megan shook her head. "They breed during the warm months of the year. They are normally in dark quiet places. It's unusual to see one out in the open like this."

"How is it you know so much about spiders?"

Megan grinned. "My boyfriend is an entomologist. I hear loads of stuff about creepy crawlies. I'll call him to remove it if you like."

"Sure. Thanks, Megan. I'm going to work on the Richfield Wedding pictures. Holler if you need me."

A couple of hours later, Megan poked her head into Darla's office. "The spider is gone. I finished the filing and confirmed the appointments for next week. How's it going in here?"

Darla leaned back in her chair and rubbed her neck. "Not great. Come look at this."

Megan peered over Darla's shoulder and pointed at the picture. "What is that?"

"It's a face, and it is in every one of these pictures from the Richfield Wedding rehearsal luncheon. At first, I thought it was just a reflection, but I change angles for different shots, so that can't be it," Darla said.

"What are you going to do? There is no way they will accept those pictures. Rehearsal luncheon? Isn't it usually a dinner?" Megan asked.

"Yes, it is usually a dinner, but when you have as much money as the Richfields, you can rehearse your wedding whenever you want. They wanted outdoor, natural light for the pictures, and the bride wanted to play croquet. I'm going to photoshop that face right out of the pictures I deliver because that is the only way we're getting paid for this mess," Darla said.

"Good idea. Hey, I'm heading out. See you tomorrow, Dar."

"Have a good night, Megan," Darla said as she reached for her phone. *Fen might know what this means or how I can start to figure it out.* Darla dialed the number of her college roommate, Fenreya Stern and was relieved when Fen answered the phone.

"Hey, Darla, what's up?" Fen said.

"Hey, Fen, the weirdest thing has happened, and I need to run it by you if you have time."

"Of course, I have time to talk to you," Fen said.

"You know how ever since the Incident and the head injury, I have been seeing dead people, but I can never hear them?"

"Yes, have you started hearing them now, too?" Fen asked.

"No, nothing like that. Oh gods, you don't think that will happen someday, do you?"

"I don't know, Dar, but what is the weird thing you called about if it isn't that?" Fen asked.

"Whenever I have seen dead folks, it has always been in person, but this time I think I captured one on film, and I didn't see them on scene when I was taking the picture. How can that even be a thing? What does it mean? Any idea how I can make it stop?" Darla asked. "Another weird thing is that other people can see the photo of the face, so maybe it's not a ghost."

"That is very strange, and I've never heard of anything like it. Can you send me a picture of it? Give me a little time to look it over and I'll call you back," Fen said.

Darla was immersed in picture fixing when the phone rang. "Hey Fen, I noticed something since we spoke. The face is looking at the bride in every picture, it's so creepy."

"I noticed that, too, and I may have an answer. While I was looking at the pictures, Michael came home, and he thought the bride looked familiar and not in a good way. He ran the picture through one of his fancy databases and she is wanted by Interpol!" Fen said.

"OMG, you're kidding me! What did she do?" Darla asked.

"Suspected of murdering a couple of her husbands, very rich husbands in Italy and France. Michael said she is what they call a 'Black Widow' and he said to tell you to keep this under wraps. The FBI has been notified, but your name was kept out of it," Fen explained.

"Okay, thanks for that. So, is the face a ghost of one of her victims?" Darla asked.

"Your guess is as good as mine, Dar. It could be a guardian angel or spirit of some kind, watching over the groom. The face did sort of hover over him the whole time it was staring at the bride. Have they seen the pictures?" Fen said.

"No, not yet. I am removing the face from the final pictures, and I don't have to deliver them until after the wedding. Jeez, the poor groom."

"He will have dodged a literal bullet once she is arrested. Call me and tell me what happens at the wedding," Fen said.

2 days later.

"Hi, Fen, I'm so glad you answered! I just got home from the 'wedding that wasn't'. I've got to fill you in," Darla said.

"Cool! I've been curious about what's going on," Fen said.

"The wedding started; everyone was waiting for the bride. Just as she started down the aisle the cops burst in and arrested her. The groom fainted and so did his mother."

Gil Miller

Gil Miller is the author of the Rural Empires series, a hard-hitting crime fiction collection that takes readers deep into the heart of small-town America. With a keen eye for detail and a deep understanding of rural life, Miller crafts stories that explore the complex relationships between power, loyalty, and justice. His novels are known for their gritty realism, morally complex characters, and the raw, unforgiving landscapes they inhabit. Whether it's a tale of corruption, survival, or betrayal, Miller's work always keeps readers on edge, questioning the line between right and wrong.

When he's not writing, Miller draws inspiration from his own experiences growing up in rural America, where he witnessed firsthand the secrets, struggles, and resilience that shape these communities. Through Rural Empires, he invites readers to explore a world where every decision carries weight and the truth is never as simple as it seems.

Desert Duel

I crouch next to a sagebrush plant in the dark, the heat radiating up from the sand and the dry, spicy smell of the desert tickling my nose. Or maybe it's a mesquite bush. How do I know? I got more serious things to worry about than identifying the local flora. As long as it hides my outline, that's all that matters.

Highway 80 lies a few yards away, snaking north out of Arizona into the western edge of New Mexico. The thought of all the heat coming off the asphalt is enough to make sweat break out on my forehead. Maybe ten yards behind me looms an old gas station, long abandoned, the old metal sign rust pitted, a faint red star on it and the letters *T* and *CO* interrupted by a large, discolored splotch.

Well, during the day, anyway. After dark, it's like everything else—mysterious and hard to see.

I'm waiting to kill something.

Off in the distance, the death scream of some small animal drifts to me on the faint breeze. I tamp down my surprise, focus on the highway. I can't afford distractions.

Some deaths are bigger than others.

The scream dies out. A minute or so later, the whisper of wings passes by overhead, crossing the highway, heading west.

And a moment after that, a shuffling noise from the south, like someone not quite picking up their feet as they walk.

I perk up.

It trudges into sight then, looking for all the world like a boy in his early teens dressed in a ragged sweatshirt and jeans, tattered dusty tennis shoes on its feet. They're of a style that went out in the seventies, those old high-topped basketball shoes. Black, of course.

It's a Black-eyed Child.

Evil bastard.

Without my even willing it, my muscles tense.

The Child shuffles on for a few more yards, head down as it apparently gazes at the ground in front of its feet.

Then it stops. It raises its head like a wolf sniffing the wind. No, not a wolf. That lends it too much dignity. Like a hyena scenting a lion.

It's onto me, but isn't sure where I am.

Moving only its head, it searches its surroundings, black eyes piercing the night. It can see in the dark far better than any human can, just like me. But it has a weakness—it can't see outlines unless you move. And thanks to its innocuous appearance, most people don't think to stop moving. Why would you? It looks like a harmless, possibly homeless, teenage boy who could use your help, if you're of a mind to give it. Maybe a ride. Maybe just a drink of water.

It's only when it gets close enough for you to see its eyes, you fear it, and by then it's too late. Their eyes are why they walk with their heads down—they're completely black, like pools of India ink. No whites, no color at all.

Give it a ride, give it a drink, and you're never seen again. One of the thousands of disappearances every year, chalked off to something as mundane as a serial killer.

What they really are, I don't know. What they do with their victims is something of a mystery, too. I don't really care, to be honest. Protecting humans is a side-effect of what I, and others like me, do. We kill Black-eyed Children because they're a blight that needs eradicating.

That means we spend a lot of time on the deserted highways Children like. Word had gone out a few days back, one had been spotted out here, and that same word has it Robert reported it.

I don't know who—or what—Robert is. He doesn't even give a name. I just call him Robert because he seems like one. Whatever he is, the Black-eyed Children avoid him if they can, and he avoids them. A bit like Tom Bombadil, he's a complete mystery, and he has powers no one can discern. He looks like a skinny guy with unruly blond hair wearing a yellow t-shirt.

I bring my mind back to the task at hand.

The Child searches the night some more, but I'm patient. I even stop pretending to breathe.

Waiting.

Finally, it moves, but more hesitantly. It's uneasy, has a feeling it's being hunted—I can tell this by how it's acting, not because I'm psychic or anything—but can't tell how close the hunter is.

Closer.

Closer.

Close enough.

I spring, grabbing for its head. If I can twist its neck, the body will die, sending it back to wherever it came from. It's a damn shame to kill the body, but the original owner is long gone.

But the Child is quick and twists aside in a way no human could ever do.

I fly past it, the element of surprise—and the opportunity of ending this quickly—gone. I wasn't counting on an easy win anyway, though it would have been nice.

I land on my feet facing it, and it's already heading for me, mouth wide open in a silent scream, eyes black pools in the night.

It's not the only one that can move fast.

I drop to my haunches, one leg sweeping out, taking the Child off its feet so it lands face-first in the sand, raising a cloud of dust. It springs back up, shaking ancient dirt loose and spitting sandy mud out of its mouth.

We're well and truly in it now.

For a moment, neither of us moves, sizing one another up. It's an old, old game.

Then it moves, becoming slightly less than a blur it's so fast, and it hits me solidly, propelling me back, bouncing me off one of the old gas pumps.

But this works in my favor. I use the rebound to bear the Child toward the highway, exerting strength, trying to bend it to my will.

Headlights pierce the darkness, coming from the south, already lighting us up. Too late to vanish into the darkness, continue this another time.

The lights must distract the Child, because it goes down, and I do my best to grind it into the pavement.

Then there's the whoop of a siren, and blue lights strobe the night. The car screeches to a halt.

I don't need this.

"Stop right there!"

Oh, how this must look. An adult assaulting a child—a *normal* child, that is—out in the middle of nowhere. Out where the cops are used to weird things happening anyway.

"Step away from the boy," the cop says.

I raise my hands. "I can't do that."

Foolish move. The Child takes advantage of it, kicks my feet out from underneath me.

I twirl in mid-air, land on my hands, use them to push myself to my feet.

All through this, the Child is scrambling away.

I follow, the cop all but forgotten. I'm too close now to let the Child get away.

That's when the cop shoots.

The bullet strikes me, its impact spinning me to the side, making me lose my momentum for a moment. But I fight back, urging my body to do things I shouldn't be doing in front of a human.

I'm acting on instinct now, though. Feet scrabbling at the asphalt, muscles straining to counteract the bullet's supersonic shockwave, I manage to stay on my feet and pursue the Child. I'm able to get a handful of sweatshirt and pull it toward me, the Child coming with it.

Another shot, but this one was ill-judged. We're twisting and turning now, and the bullet catches the Child in the middle of the back, bursting out of its chest in a spray of gore.

The body goes limp, what made the Child a Child instantly gone as the vessel is destroyed.

"I said stop!" There's panic in the cop's voice now, but the night is only going to get worse for him.

I can't stay around.

Relaxing my hand, I let the body fall to the edge of the highway, then turn and jump out of the cone of headlights, bounding to the roof of the gas station. I pause there and exert my will. I still have a bullet lodged in my body, and I need to get it out. It takes some effort—and more than a little pain—but I force it out. It drops to the roof with a thump.

The cop is on the radio now. It'll be some time before any backup can make it here, but this close to the Mexican border, it'll be more than just police. I can't afford to stick around, see what happens. The Child is gone anyway, which is all I wanted.

I glance at the body lying in the wash of headlights, but the Child won't be able to salvage it, make use of it again. I jump to the ground on the opposite side of the building from the officer and fade into the desert.

My job is done here. There'll be others, though. There always are. Some other empty road, some other deserted place, world without end, amen.

This battle is over. The war continues.

My Summer Vacation

Well, this all started cause my dad's a ghost catcher. It's a little like being a cop or a dogcatcher, except he catches ghosts. He always gripes that it don't pay well, and when Mom asks why he doesn't get a different job then, he says cause he couldn't stand another one. And then they don't talk for a while, and I don't like that.

Anyway, part of what Dad does is kinda like you see in *Ghostbusters*. He has these traps he uses to catch the ghosts. Most of the time, he takes them back to the place he works. They do something with them there, I don't know what, and Dad brings back empty traps for next time. I asked him one time what they do but didn't understand it. Maybe when I grow up.

So anyways, there was this one time about halfway through the summer. I was getting bored cause most of my friends were gone to places like Florida or Hawaii and I didn't have anything to do. It was hot outside, and I'd played all my video games and stuff, and Mom wouldn't get me any more. Our lawn mower didn't work very good, so I couldn't mow lawns for money and buy my own.

So I got stuck at home watching shows on Cartoon Network and Nickelodeon. Boring. I'd seen all of them. And I hate SpongeBob. *Hate* him.

I didn't think nothing of it when Dad left for work that morning. I was still in bed. He went to other states sometimes to work, and he'd just got back from Georgia or somewhere like that and spent the night at the house. I didn't get to see much of him cause him and Mom drank some wine and started acting silly. Then they sent me to bed and I knew what was up and turned my TV up really loud for a while. Then I went to sleep and when I woke up Dad was already gone. Mom said he'd be back later to take me to the park or a movie or something, so that was cool.

So I was lying on the couch, throwing a ball up in the air, almost bouncing it off the ceiling. The TV was off cause I got tired of listening to SpongeBob and his dorky friends do stupid stuff. Those cartoons are only funny when you're a little kid. Mom was off at the hairdresser and stuff. She says that since I'm 11 now I can be at home by myself for a while. That's okay. I like it sometimes. Wish I had a little brother, but I don't think that's going to happen.

The house was pretty quiet. I threw the ball, almost touching the ceiling. That was the trick, to get it as close as I could without touching it. A lawn mower buzzed down the block. Probably some kid making money for a new game.

Then came a scratching noise at the back door. That was Barney, our golden retriever. Maybe I could get him to play with me. I went and opened the door to let him in. He came in with his tail going like crazy and tried to lick me, but I pushed him away. He went over to his dish and drank some water. I went back in the living room to look for Barney's ball. He has this tennis ball he loves. I'd have to take him outside, though, or I'd get in trouble for messing up the house. Even when I didn't break nothing, it seemed like Mom knew I'd been playing ball in the house and I got in trouble.

The ball was under the edge of the couch. Barney came in the living room, on his way to his bed by the front door. I couldn't help it. I threw the ball to him. He bounced up in the air and caught it, then banged into the table by the front door on his way back down.

One of Dad's ghost traps was there. He must have forgot it when he went to work. It fell under Barney and the next thing I knew I was hearing this weird hissing sound.

That's when the ghost came out.

I wasn't really very scared. I've been with Dad on a couple of his jobs, and he says most ghosts won't hurt you. They just do scary things to get your attention. Dad says most ghosts are just people who died and don't really know it yet, that all he does is show them they're dead and they need to move on. He's been a ghost catcher for a long time, so I guess he knows what he's talking about.

But I always noticed he said *most* ghosts.

I don't think this was one of those kind.

I never did see it really good, so I don't know what it looked like. I know it didn't look like no lost little boy like Dad said he found one time. And it made an awful sound when it came out of the trap. Barney howled once and went somewhere and hid. I don't know where he went to. Wherever it was, he didn't come out till late that night.

The ghost went flying out of the trap and the first thing it did was knock a picture off the wall.

Oh, man. Mom was gonna kill me for sure.

The ghost went through the wall and disappeared.

What was I gonna do? I didn't know how to trap a ghost. Dad didn't use one of those backpack thingies they do on *Ghostbusters,* but he had to have something. Whatever it was, he took it with him. Then something broke in the next room. That was Mom and Dad's bedroom. I was toast.

I looked at the trap and tried to think. How would you trap a ghost?

How was I supposed to know? I was just a kid. Not a *little* kid, but still a kid. I didn't know nothing about trapping ghosts. I had to figure it out, though. This ghost had already broken two things, and I was gonna be in trouble. If I didn't get it trapped, it would tear up the whole house.

I looked at the trap. It didn't look like the *Ghostbusters* kind. It was just a square metal box with a thing on top that looked like the electric burner on Mom's stove, but smaller. Right now, that burner thing was glowing red. There were two buttons and a dial beside the burner thingy. The dial looked like it had come from a stove, too.

The dial was turned to the left. And the buttons were red and green. The red one was pushed in. I looked at it for a minute. If that's all it had, it must not be hard to use.

Yeah! That made sense! Dad said sometimes you don't have much time to catch a ghost. So, the trap must not be hard to use.

If the red button was pushed in, what happened if you pushed the green one? Or did I need to turn the dial first? I was afraid to call Dad. Maybe I could catch this ghost before it broke too much. Yeah.

I pushed the green button, but nothing happened. The red one stayed pushed in and the green one popped back out. So I turned the dial. It clicked all the way over to the right and the red button popped out. Cool! I pushed the green button and it stayed in. The burner-looking thingy turned green and the trap started humming. It sounded like one of those big overhead electric lines.

What was I supposed to do now, though? Did I pick it up and take it with me?

I looked around. No ghost. So the trap must not bring the ghost back.

I picked up the trap. It was a little cold, like it had been in the refrigerator, but it was no big deal. Now, where was the ghost? Last place I heard it was in Mom and Dad's room, so I went there.

Mom's lamp was on the floor, broke in about a million pieces. Some of the wires inside it stuck out. Would have been neat except I was going to be in trouble.

Or would I? Dad would know he'd left the trap at home. I couldn't let the ghost run around breaking things, but at least he'd know he left the trap, so maybe they'd know it wasn't my fault.

I looked around the room. Nothing else was broke. No ghost, either. How do you find something that goes through walls? And Dad said some of them are invisible. Oh, boy. This was tough.

Maybe the ghost was hiding.

Yeah! Maybe that was it! It had been in this trap once already. Maybe it didn't want to go back. I looked down at the trap. If the ghost wouldn't come to it, and would run away from me if I carried the thing with me, what was I gonna do?

I'd have to set up a trap, like on *Scooby Doo*.

No, that was stupid. All the monsters on *Scooby Doo* always turned out to be real people dressed up like monsters. They were always trying to scare people away from gold or something. This was a real ghost and it wouldn't care about gold or any of that. And the only thing it seemed afraid of was the trap. If I had another trap, I might set up something….

That's when I remembered the old trap Dad had in the garage. It was a dummy, he told me, and they used it to train new ghost catchers. The real traps could be dangerous, so they used these fake ones. But it looked real.

Something broke in the kitchen and I groaned.

Okay. I had to stay calm. Where should I put this trap? It could go through walls, so that made it harder to figure. If I used the dummy trap, the ghost might go out the front wall into the yard, or up in the attic crawlspace or something. Would the trap catch it if it got close enough?

Dang, I needed Dad here.

No. I was 11. I could figure this out.

Oh, man. The ghost was in the kitchen. And I'd have to go through there to get the dummy trap. That would scare the ghost off in some other direction.

Well, maybe not. I could go ahead and put the trap in the middle of the living room. You couldn't see the kitchen from there 'cause of the dining room. Then I could go out a window and go around to the garage and get the dummy trap and come back in through the kitchen door. That might work!

Back in the living room, I moved the coffee table from in front of the couch and put the trap on the floor halfway between the couch and the TV. That was close to the middle of the room. Then I went to my room and climbed out the window.

Good thing my bedroom was on the back of the house where my neighbors couldn't see me.

I snuck inside the garage. It was dim in there, but I couldn't raise the door or the ghost would know I was in here. But where was the dummy trap? I hadn't seen it in a while. I hoped Dad hadn't taken it back to work.

Then I saw it on a shelf, just as I heard a huge crash from inside the house. Oh no. Mom's China cabinet in the dining room.

For a moment I stood there in the garage, smelling the sawdust from Dad's woodworking projects. Maybe I should just stay out here, let the ghost tear everything up. If Mom came home and found me in the garage, she'd know I didn't do it, wouldn't she?

But wait a minute. This was my house. What if it got in my room and tore up some of my stuff? What if it broke my Xbox 360? I almost didn't get that bought for me. No ghost was gonna break it!

I got mad.

I grabbed the dummy trap and went through the door into the kitchen. Mom's cookie jar was on the floor, chocolate chip cookies scattered all over. Some of the plates were out of the cabinets, and there were pieces of glass everywhere. When had this happened? Must have been while I was outside.

Stupid ghost.

"Why don't you go to somebody else's house, stupid? Why don't you just go away and not come back?"

I don't know why I did that. Just wanted to yell at something. At the ghost.

It was real quiet for a minute. Then something else crashed. It was still in the dining room. Mom had lots of breakable stuff in there. I couldn't go in there when I was a little kid. And now the ghost was breaking everything.

I held the dummy trap out in front of me, so the ghost would be able to see it, and went into the dining room. I could see it there, or part of it, looking like some old raggedy sheet or something, except you could see through it. I held the dummy trap up higher. The ghost stopped what it was doing, then went through the wall. Back into the kitchen.

Dang it!

I ran back into the kitchen, but it wasn't there. I didn't stop but ran into the garage. No ghost there, either.

What the heck?

I went out the side door, and there it was in the back yard. As soon as it saw me, it went back through the wall and into the house. Before I could even get back in, I heard something else break.

I ran into the living room and saw the TV, a new flat screen Mom and Dad had bought with their tax money, laying on the floor. There were pictures off the walls, and even stuffing torn out of the couch. But I didn't see the ghost anywhere.

I looked at the trap on the floor. The green light was blinking, and the burner thingy was dark. The ghost was back in the trap. I walked over and picked it up. It was really cold now. More like it had been in the freezer.

Then Mom's car pulled up in the driveway. A minute later she opened the door. I stood there holding the dummy trap.

Mom stopped inside the door and looked at the mess, her eyes big and round.

"Brian," she said, her voice real quiet, "what did you do?"

Oh, boy. This was going to be worse than acting like the dog ate my homework.

The Big Scam

She closed the book, placed it on the table, and *finally* decided to walk through the door.

I sighed in relief. Thought she'd never build up the courage.

I watched from inside the utility closet. I couldn't see into the inner office. The scam was all on her. All I could do was wait.

Could she pull it off? Danny Forelli was a tough customer. The office might look legit, and Forelli ran the brokerage that way. But he was dirty. Everybody that counted knew it. That's why we decided to pull the Big Scam on him.

Anna had worked for him about six months, posing as a new accountant. She was a *forensic* accountant, and the book was a ledger. Hard to believe it these days, but Forelli kept the really important numbers—important to *us,* anyway—on treeware. I'd driven myself crazy trying to find something in his corporate system, but there was nothing. Encrypted files, sure, but nothing incriminating. I broke into them easily, backed out without leaving tracks. Standard company secrets. Client data. That sort of thing.

But I wanted the Big Score. The gift that kept on giving. Forelli had too much to lose to let info like this out. The *real* numbers, the ones that kept track of where his dirty cash came from. Forelli had his fingers in a lot of pies.

I wasn't sure how or where Anna found that ledger. And

even if it seemed old-fashioned at first, the more I thought about it, the more it made sense. You can't hack treeware, only find it. I have *years* of computer schooling and experience. Could be a top IT person at any Fortune 500 company. But where's the fun in that? Solving problems all the users manage to cause? Please. Too many ulcers and too few rewards.

So I hack. And I scam. Sometimes I even take on a partner.

I took out my iPhone, checked the time. Had it really only been five minutes?

It was stuffy in the closet. They needed to fix the air-conditioning in this place. Maybe get someone in here to clean the ducts. Air flow wasn't so good.

I had all kinds of gadgets that would have let me see into Forelli's office, but he had security out the wazoo. Too risky. If Anna had so much as worn a wire in, the alarms would have gone off. She even had to leave her phone outside.

C'mon, Anna. Get the payoff so we can go somewhere tropical and have umbrella drinks in funny colors. Sit on the beach, watch the waves. This scam could set us up for life, and she would be a good one to have a life with. Smart. Pretty. I might even be in love.

I looked at the book where it lay on the table.

Wait a minute. The book. I'd been so nervous I hadn't hit on it before. Why had she left the book? It was the proof we needed.

Was she betraying me?

It lay there, looking like something from another age.

That's when I heard the yell. And the shot. Both were muffled, but obvious. A twinge in my chest, a moment of sadness for Anna.

I closed the door to the closet, climbed up through the ventilation duct.

It was sad, really, but that was life. This one hadn't

worked, and I'd miss Anna. But it was just a job. She knew it just like I had.

Time to move on to the next one.

Tim Ritter

A native of Springfield, Missouri, Tim Ritter grew up in a performing family and discovered writing and public speaking early in life. By age 13, his writings included poetry, two children's adventure books, several plays and a comic strip which eventually found its way to his junior high school newspaper. He also discovered that he liked being on stage, and how people tended to listen when he spoke into a microphone.

Throughout his 29-year professional career as a mechanical engineer, Tim wrote articles for trade magazines and was the featured speaker at hundreds of seminars across the country. Now in what he calls "rewirement", his published books have included both fiction and nonfiction.

Tim lives outside Fair Grove, Missouri, with his wife, Lisa, writing full-time and speaking to retirement facilities, civic groups, and organizations on a variety of topics. In addition to being past president of the Springfield Writers Guild, he is a member of Sleuths' Ink Mystery Writers, the historical societies in Douglas, Christian, and Polk Counties, Ozarks Genealogical Society, and the Poe Studies Association.

Phobia

"I'm afraid of heights. Are you afraid of anything?"

Eli turned and looked at the man next to him at the bar. Sitting there in silence for several minutes, he was surprised by the sudden bizarre question from the stranger.

The man turned and looked at him.

"So, are you afraid of anything?"

"Not really," Eli answered blandly.

"Nothing? You're not afraid of anything?"

"Well, maybe this qualifies: I'm terribly claustrophobic. I hate tight spaces."

"Yeah." The man nodded. "That's a good one."

The two men fell silent again.

Eli called the bartender over.

"I'm heading for the bathroom. If no one else takes my seat while I'm gone, set me up with another bourbon. Neat."

When he returned from the bathroom, his seat was still open, and a glass of bourbon awaited him.

As he settled in and picked up the glass to drink, the man next to him spoke up again.

"Cheers!" He raised his glass as Eli took a sip. "Here's to claustrophobia."

Eli gave him a puzzled look as a slight grin crept across the man's face.

Within seconds, Eli's eyelids felt heavy.

"Oh shit," he whispered as everything went black.

Eli's eyes wouldn't open. His mind felt sluggish, as if he had been asleep for days. Every breath felt like a chore, and his heart thumped hard but slowly.

As the seconds ticked by, he became aware of two things: he couldn't see, and he couldn't move. He wanted to move. His fingers and toes could move, but his ankles and wrists were confined, taped or strapped. His nose itched and he wanted to scratch it.

Taking stock of his situation, he could tell he was sitting in a chair and was strapped to it. He couldn't move his legs or his upper torso.

Worst of all, his head was taped up completely, except for his nostrils and his ears. Everything else was taped over. His eyes and his mouth were completely taped shut, and his head was strapped or taped to the chair.

Dammit. That guy put something in my drink. Thanks for asking me what I was afraid of, asshole.

He tried to remain calm.

Okay, so now what? This guy most likely stole my money and my identification while I was out. What else does he want with me? Does he want me to be scared? I'm restrained, but I can't tell if I'm in a small space or a warehouse. Stay calm, Eli. It's a warehouse. You got this.

A nearby door opened then closed. He heard quiet footsteps approach.

I was right. It's a big room.

The footsteps approached and walked around him a couple of times.

He is watching me, to see if I'm scared. Might wonder if I'm breathing hard. Guess what, asshole! I'm not! Failed this one!

The footsteps stopped. Eli strained to listen. He knew the person was still there. He heard faint noises, something moving. Then he felt a quick pain, like a pinprick. Then sleepiness again.

Eli blinked a couple of times as he regained consciousness. His eyes couldn't focus. His mind again felt sluggish, as if he had been asleep for days. The tape around his head was gone. He could breathe, albeit laboriously, through his mouth and could almost hear his heart thumping.

A few more blinks, and he felt like he could keep his eyes open. But once again, his body could not move. His arms and his legs were completely pinned down. He tried to move his hands and feet, but he could not. Only his head moved.

The sheet. The sheet covering him – he guessed it was a sheet – was so tight over him he could barely breathe. Tiny drops of sweat began to break out on his forehead.

The room was completely dark. Had he been able to move, he could not have seen his hand in front of his face.

Why the hell is this thing so tight? It doesn't feel like cloth. Congratulations. I'm once again confined.

A door opened, then latched closed. He heard footsteps.

"Hey!" Eli called out, his voice raspy.

The footsteps stopped. Whoever was in the blackened room, they heard him.

"Hey, can you please help me here? I…I can't move. This is really uncomfortable."

The footsteps moved again, closer to him, then a few steps away.

Another door opened, then closed. It didn't sound like the first one.

He didn't hear anymore footsteps.

Suddenly there was bright white light everywhere. Eli squeezed shut his stinging eyes as they began to water. He blinked a few times, wishing he could move his arms so he could wipe his eyes. A couple more blinks, and he was able to slowly open his eyes, squinting at first, then opening all the way, to discover his surroundings.

What the hell?

He was in a tight circular enclosure. Like a small lighted tunnel of some sort. He could tell he was lying on a hard surface, and the material covering him was a white rubbery sheet, stretched tight over him. His arms were pressed up against his sides, and the only thing he could move, aside from his head, was his fingers. He could wiggle them just a little.

Then the thing, the tube he was in, began to roar as he noticed little bars of light rotate over him. To his horror, he realized his situation.

My God, I'm strapped down in some kind of machine, like an MRI.

Eli was not a stranger to an MRI. He had been scanned before, after an injury while playing football. But he hadn't been restrained like this, nor had he awakened inside the machine with no explanation.

Who the hell is this guy? Why am I here? What has happened to me?

"Hey! Hey, I know you can hear me! Why am I here? What has happened to me?"

His heart pounded and he dripped with sweat. He could not hear anything over the roar of the machine as the little bars of light rotated faster over him.

The area of the tube directly over his face lit up bright white, then faded to reveal a monitor. It only took a moment for Eli to realize he was being shown the scan of his body in real time. He could see everything from head to toe.

Then he saw it. In the area of his abdomen. A black mass. It had no discernable shape. He couldn't really make out what organs it was near. But it was clearly a mass. And it was moving. He couldn't feel it, but it was moving inside him.

Holy shit!

"Hey! Get me out of here! What the hell is this thing

moving around in me? Hey, can you hear me?"

The screen went dark, and the machine began to wind down, finally ending its rotation. The table upon which he lay began to slide out of the machine, and Eli felt cool air on his sweat-drenched face for the first time since he awakened. He longed to move his arms and wipe the sweat from his face and hoped whoever was in the control room would soon come out and free him from the sheet restricting him so intensely.

But no.

Just as he began to calm down, the table began to slowly slide back into the machine. Eli closed his eyes and tried to keep from hyperventilating as he slipped deeper and deeper into the narrow tube.

Relax, Eli, relax.

He tried to calm himself down, but at this point, all he could think about was getting out of the tube and out from under the sheet.

The tube began to rotate over him, and the screen lit up again. This time it showed just his abdomen area, and the moving mass. Eli looked closely. The mass churned and moved, almost like a heavy viscous fluid. Then he saw it. An arm.

He couldn't hold back a scream.

"What the hell is this? Somebody answer me!"

The machine wound down again as the screen went black. The table began to move him out again, slower than the first time.

These people are clearly screwing with me.

Taking what felt like an agonizing sixty seconds, the table finally cleared the machine, and Eli was out in the fresh air. He laid still, drenched with sweat, looking around to see if anyone was coming to set him free.

The lights went out again, plunging the room into complete darkness. He heard a door open and close, and footsteps approaching from behind him.

Must be whoever was in the control room. Better not say anything too hateful. They might stick me back in that goddamn thing.

He lay quietly, waiting for whatever happened next. Suddenly he felt a sharp pain in his neck, as if he had been stuck with something again.

Then everything went black.

Eli began to awaken, again lying down. This time it felt softer, and in his clouded mind he detected no restraint. He opened his eyes and sat up quickly.

“Easy there, Eli, don’t sit up too fast. Take your time.”

The voice was male, deep, and soothing. Eli rubbed his eyes, happy to be able to move his arms. He ran his hands over his face, dropped his arms, and opened his eyes.

He was in an office. Fine oak bookcases lined the walls. A large oak desk sat to his left, and across the room, in a plush high-backed chair, sat a man.

Eli looked closely at him. He was the man from the bar who asked him what he was afraid of. Clearly the man knew his name, but otherwise, Eli had no idea who he was. With dark, swept-back hair, large plastic-rimmed glasses, the man sat upright in his chair looking at Eli with a slight grin.

“Who are you?” Eli asked.

“I’m Doctor William Sperry. Welcome to my research project.”

“Research project? I never agreed to be part of any project! You slipped something into my drink at the bar and then kidnapped me!”

Doctor Sperry looked at Eli for a moment.

“On the contrary. Just before you passed out at the bar, I asked you if you’d like me to take you somewhere. You nodded. So, you see, you consented.”

“You waited until I was under the influence of whatever you gave me…”

“Sodium pentothal.”

"… sodium whatever. I think your constituents would consider such activity quite illegal."

"That may be true if I had constituents. I work independently."

Eli stopped for a moment and scratched his head.

"What was that machine, and that thing inside me?"

"Thing inside you?" Dr. Sperry looked puzzled.

"When I was in that MRI thing. On the screen. It showed me a mass in my stomach."

Eli reached down and lifted his shirt, looking for an incision. There were no signs of anything. Just his skin.

"Perhaps the relaxant made you see things." Dr. Sperry scribbled a note on his phone.

"I don't know what you gave me, but clearly the screen showed me a mass. And it had an arm or leg or something. It was moving, though I didn't feel it."

"Don't worry, Eli. You're fine."

"Okay, if I'm fine, would you mind telling me why you did those things to me?"

"I'm studying reactions to phobias, how people act when they face their fears, or when they think they are facing their fears."

"So that's why you had me taped up but in a big room."

"You could tell you were in a big room?"

"Yeah. Your footsteps and the echo gave it away. I was confined, but I knew I wasn't in a small space. So it didn't bother me as much as the machine did."

"Interesting. I have to make a note of that." Sperry wrote more notes on his phone. Eli watched as the doctor mouthed the note he was typing.

This guy is completely nuts.

"Would you like something to drink, Eli?"

Doctor Sperry got up and walked to a cabinet, opening the door to reveal a refrigerator stocked with various soft drinks and bottles of water.

"At this point I'd really like some water."

Sperry grabbed a bottle of water and set it down on the shelf above the refrigerator. He turned his back to Eli to remove the lid, then turned around and brought the water to him.

"Enjoy. I'm sure you're thirsty."

Eli jumped up and tackled Sperry and pinned him to the floor.

"What were you planning to do, *Doctor*?" Eli snidely emphasized the word. "What did you put in my water when you turned your back to me?"

"I didn't put anything in your water." Sperry struggled to get up but couldn't move.

"Oh really? Then you won't mind drinking it yourself!"

Eli shoved the water bottle into Sperry's mouth, squeezing it to force the water in. He then threw the empty bottle across the room and covered Sperry's mouth to force him to swallow it.

Within seconds, Sperry's eyes got heavy, and he was soon unconscious.

A man's remains were found at the base of a tall transmission tower, discovered by the farmer whose land the structure stood upon. When the sheriff began investigating the grisly scene, he found the man to be void of any wallet or identification. Searching further, a piece of paper was found in the man's shirt. A simple message was scrawled on the sheet.

"So, Doctor, you're afraid of heights?"

Ana Glenn

Ana Glenn, as the oldest child, always felt responsible to help and teach others. She expresses this in her short stories and poetry.

She is an award-winning author of short stories, a former automotive dealership accounting leader, trainer and consultant, real estate manager, and auto racer. She is returning to her first love- writing. She rediscovered love with her childhood sweetheart, James in 2020. Open heart surgery paused her writing for over a year and now she returns to her first passion. Her main passion is, as always, her growing family which now includes four great grandchildren. Since retirement she enjoys visiting her family in Missouri, Massachusetts, and Florida.

Daddy's Gun

It was a stifling hot, late September day in Fresno, California, the year I turned thirteen. We had no air conditioning, and the few fans in the hallway did little to relieve the oppressive heat. Momma had just finished a long breakfast/lunch shift at the Ramada Inn restaurant.

Daddy had driven to pick her up since she did not drive and was not supposed to work yet. She had an emergency medical procedure just a short week before, and the hospital doctor adamantly instructed her not to work for a minimum of four weeks. In addition, he instructed her to lift nothing over a five-pound bag of flour and no sex in that time.

They came into the house arguing, or as usual, Daddy was complaining to Momma, as she was trying to say something. Their "conversations" had increasingly become angrier the more Daddy drank. Since he wasn't working, he had a beer in his hand from the time he woke up until he eventually passed out. My sisters and I tried so hard to stay out of his way and not anger him, just like Momma did.

Lately, it had taken more work. He was "on leave" from his security guard job and was incredibly angry about the two weeks off without pay. I never found out what that was all about. All I knew was that, as usual in their fourteen years of marriage, Momma was our family's financial support.

"Get outside and play now!" Daddy yelled to us as he

pushed Momma down the hallway toward their bedroom. I heard the door slam, and the yelling continued. I had always felt protective of Momma and was worried about her safety. I crept down the hallway and stood outside the closed door. I could hear Momma pleading to him, "Please, Herb, I just need to lie down. I'm tired, I'm hurting bad, and bleeding again. Please let me rest and just go away!"

I heard him swear, and then a hard slap. That's when I opened the door and saw him standing over her with his 38-revolver pointed at her. His contorted mouth growled at her. "Do as I say now, or I'll kill you and those girls."

Momma meekly said, "Okay, just put the gun down, please." I watched him place it on the bedside table and return to Momma.

He never heard me open the door or move toward the bedside table. He was too busy swearing and screaming at Momma. Momma saw me as I raised the gun toward him. "No, Anna, he's not worth ruining your life!" He leapt towards me, but I was just out of his reach. He stopped dead in his tracks as I cocked the hammer back, and I still remember the sobering look of shock on his face.

He and Momma both were pleading with me to put down the gun. I was suddenly fearful that if I put the gun down, he would kill me right then, and Momma and my little sisters would be next. I had suffered so much abuse and a multitude of beatings at his hand, so I fully knew what he was capable of. I had witnessed too many beatings of my Momma and sisters, and something in me just snapped.

Momma gently came over and placed her hands over mine, softly telling me, "He won't hurt you or me. He will leave the house and sober up. Your future is worth so much; don't end it now."

He left the house for about an hour. Momma and I talked briefly, and she explained she understood why I did what I did and how wrong it was. She also explained I should never do anything like it again. I later heard him tell Momma they should call Juvenile Hall and have me removed from the house as dangerous. He changed his mind when Momma asked him if he really wanted me to tell the authorities my story.

I don't know if I would have pulled the trigger. It was as if I was watching things happen in a movie, and it was not me standing there with the gun. Daddy's gun was never left sitting around again, and a month later, he took off again for unknown parts. My entire childhood, his pattern was to arrive and stay five or six months, then abruptly leave for months or more at a time. When I was younger, I wondered what I had done to make my daddy leave us. After this, I realized his immaturity and inability to manage the responsibility of a wife and children were the problem.

DREAM MAN

My thirty-year-old daughter, Heather, in utter disbelief, yelled at me, "Mother, you did what?"

I repeated my prior statement. "I met the man I've been seeing in my dreams. He really exists, and I met him today! He has the same warm smile and blue laughing eyes I came to know in my dreams. He's even more handsome than in my dreams because his whole body lit up when we made eye contact and smiled at each other. It was as if we knew each other all our lives, at least for me.

"He's tall, and a working man's muscles rippled under his pale blue denim shirt. His strong legs were apparent under his perfectly fitted jeans. Sparks flew when he wrapped his strong arms around me and asked if I was okay. I was trembling as he gently held me, but not because of the gunman who had just minutes earlier threatened to kill me if I moved and didn't give him my purse and jewelry. My quaking was because of the intensity of the fire his touch generated in my body as he held me in his strong arms to comfort me."

Only minutes earlier, I had been trembling from the fright of unexpected danger while contemplating how to comply with the gunman's demands and guarantee he would just leave with my possessions and not kill me or worse. Suddenly, this kind and compassionate man who had guided me through so many night journeys in my dreams appeared from nowhere to grab my assailant and throw him to the ground. The thug's gun sailed from his hand as he was knocked to the pavement, and with one well-placed blow, rendered unconscious. My dream rescuer retrieved the weapon and placed it in his belt behind the huge silver eagle buckle, and all I could say was thank you, thank you, as tears gently rolled down my cheeks. I'm sure he thought my tears were from fear and the release of it. Little did he know they were tears of joy that this wonderful man I'd seen in my dreams for years was real, and he was holding me now.

"Mother, you were robbed at gunpoint, and all you can talk about is the man from your dreams. Are you crazy?"

Yes, I was robbed, or at least the POS attempted to. It scared me and made me angry at the same time, but I knew I'd be safe because God always walks with me. I just didn't think I'd meet the man who had been guiding me through struggles in my dreams. He was in the background of dozens of dreams over the last few years.

The first time was in the nightmare after Dad's suicide when I didn't know how I'd continue and was racked with guilt. He was there, comforting arms engulfing me, telling me softly, that everything will be okay, cry, grieve, be angry, it's all okay. There was nothing I could have done. I felt peace as I awoke.

The last time was months ago after breaking off my engagement with the masterful prevaricator. I forgave his betrayal of my trust and the months of lies and deceit. I genuinely believed he was remorseful and had changed until the old signs reappeared and the dreams began again. This time, he was professing his love as he repeated the words, I know you love me, as a mantra.

When I walked away, I knew it would be the last time I'd be with him. It was his final admission of lying to an innocent question and his anger at my questioning his truthfulness. It was the final uncomfortable conversation for him; he just didn't realize it yet. I had no doubt he had finally killed my love with this final deceit and futile attempt at justifying his "innocent" lies to protect me. He said he needed time to think before giving me a decision on whether we'd move forward and how he'd forgive me. Little did he know I reached my decision regardless of his choice. It was over a week later when I received his hesitant call that we could work this out with his few conditions.

He required no more uncomfortable conversations, and he promised not to have physical intimacy with others. I let him recite his demands and calmly told him to save them for the next woman in his life because I deserved and demanded better than that. I calmly wished him well, and he said he wanted to remain a dear friend and talk from time to time. And like before, he hoped I could see we were meant to be together because he's a good man, and at my age, a good man is hard to find. Once again, I allowed a seed of doubt and fear of aloneness to enter my mind. Am I making a mistake?

That night, my dream friend appeared and took my hand. We walked down a beautiful path bordered by majestic oak trees, and I caught glimpses along the way of the most painful events of my life. He held my hand firmly yet gently at the same time, and when I would flinch at a memory, he gently squeezed it and smiled at me. No words spoken. I felt comforted and at peace with the pain of the past and ready to move forward unencumbered by it. When I awoke, I felt calm and believed he was my guardian angel and could not be a living, breathing man.

"My dear daughter, today, I met my guardian angel as a flesh and blood man who looked at me with kind, compassionate baby blue eyes. Tomorrow, at lunch, I'll learn more about him with my eyes, mind, and heart open to whatever the future holds for me with him. Just wish me a joyful and love-filled life and know whatever the future holds, I'll be more than okay."

I do hope he and my experience are real and not a dream.

THE WEDDING PHOTOGRAPHER

Hi, I'm Teresa Hamby, wedding photographer extraordinaire, and this is my first "ghost" figure. From the very beginning, this wedding has been different from any other in my twenty-year worldwide career. The proofs I just reviewed for this wedding couple take them to a whole new level. Every picture of the happy couple has a shadowy figure behind the groom, with his gaze laser focused on the bride. The figure doesn't appear in any of the thousands of other shots. I photographed Mrs. Anna Stark, one of the most captivating brides I've worked with. Her life is full of fascinating stories, and she is one of the kindest clients I've had the opportunity to work with. It's clear to all that she and James are devoted and deeply in love.

Their love story is the most interesting one she told. Anna has lived in Polk County for just over five years. Her first three years were a nightmare after her husband, Sam, disappeared. Local folks speculated on how she murdered and disposed of his body. There was renewed controversy when she and James, the deputy investigating the case, began dating a year ago. There was no evidence of foul play, and Sam was declared dead six months ago. Their families and friends all said there was no way Anna would ever harm Sam, and he must be deceased to have disappeared without a word. Anna rarely spoke of Sam, and when she did, it was always with a sense of great sadness.

It occurred to me that the figure resembled Sam. As her friend and photographer, I must show her the unretouched photos.

My hands tremble as I punch her number into the phone. I don't know what to say or how to tell her what she needs to see. When I hear her happy voice, I hesitate to tell her I have something she needs to see. We arrange to meet in an hour to discuss the photos.

When she arrives, James is by her side. Anna felt something was wrong and wanted his support. We sit down to view the photos, and Anna gasps when she sees the first one. She shrieks, "It's Sam! That's impossible! He was not there! How is this possible? Was he in all the pictures?"

I calmly say, "He was not there and is in none of the other pictures. Only the ones of you and James. What do you think this means? I've never taken any photos of Sam."

Anna slumps and says, "Sam is really dead... this proves it to me. It's his way of saying goodbye to me and approving of James and me being together. I guess whatever or whoever he was running from finally caught up with him and killed him. Sam once mentioned that terrifying people wanted him dead. He would never say anything else. He didn't want to endanger me or our families."

She did not tell me she would later embark on a quest to discover why and how he was murdered. I would soon learn Anna is convinced Sam is dead and his body just hasn't been found and identified. I have a feeling Anna Stark is relentless once she sets her mind to something.

We discussed the photos, and I printed an unretouched set for her and gave her the negatives. I then printed the retouched images for her family albums. This is a story I may share in the future, but for now, I will only share it here in my diary. I don't want anyone to figure out my role in Sam's demise yet. After all, I am the reason he no longer walks the earth but resides beneath it.

Margarite Stever

Margarite Stever is an award-winning author who grew up in Asbury, a tiny Missouri town of just over 200 people. Though she now lives in a much larger city, she stays true to her roots. She has a Bachelor of Arts Degree in English from Missouri Southern State University.

She is a member of Joplin Writers' Guild, Missouri Writers Guild, Sleuths' Ink Mystery Writers, and serves on the boards of Ozarks Writers League and Ozarks Romance Authors.

She has published two books, *Sally's Secret Legacy*, and *Moonbeams and Ashes*. Her work has appeared in several journals, magazines, and anthologies including: *Romance, Poetry, Mystery and More: An Anthology by Ozarks Romance Authors Members, Chicken Soup for the Soul: It's Beginning to Look a Lot Like Christmas, Seasons of the Four States, Anthology 2019 Sleuths' Ink Mystery Writers*,

Missouri's Emerging Writers, Legends: Passion Pages, 50-Word Stories website, and *Writer's Digest: Show Us Your Shorts.*

You can visit her website at www.margaritestever.com. Her seeds of wisdom and joy can be seen on her blog at http://ozarksmaven.com.

Nightcaps and Nightshade

Thunder boomed, rattling the windows of the police department as I trudged to the breakroom. Leaning against the counter, a muscular officer with short brown hair blocked access to the coffee pot.

"Excuse me," I said holding up my empty mug.

"Sorry." He grinned. "I don't want to keep you from your liquid energy."

I smiled at his obvious effort at charm and filled my mug. "I'm Grace Sanders. You must be the new sergeant."

"Levi Cornell, but you can call me Sarge."

I took a healthy gulp of coffee.

"You're the overnight dispatcher?" he asked.

"I'm the records clerk, but I volunteered to work tonight because we're short-handed." I yawned and glanced at the clock. "Midnight. I'm usually in bed by now."

Another thunderclap shook the windows. "You wouldn't be getting much sleep if you were."

"You're right about that." I stifled another yawn.

His radio crackled. I waved at him and returned to dispatch while he answered it.

A couple of months passed with only brief interactions until one morning I found him in my office.

"Good morning, Sarge. What brings you to my little piece of paradise?"

"I need your help. Would you see if you can find anything about local deaths involving poison for me? Any unsolved deaths, too."

"What timeframe?"

"The past fifty years."

"Fifty?" I sat back in my chair, my mouth agape.

He nodded. "Yeah. It's a hunch. Nathaniel Combs was found dead in his greenhouse three weeks ago. The picture of good health. Jogged every day. Lab reports indicate he was poisoned. He's not the first poisoning case we've had either. We may have a serial killer on our hands."

"What makes you think so?"

"Levi, are you back here?" a female voice called, cutting off his reply.

"In Records, Aunt Sue," he answered.

An older woman sauntered into my office like she owned it, ignoring me. "There you are. Ready for breakfast?"

"Just finishing up here," Sarge said.

The woman raked her gaze over me for the first time. "You must be new. I'm Sue MacAlister, Levi's aunt. I used to be the head dispatcher here. I ran this place for over twenty years."

I forced a smile. "Grace Sanders. I'm the records clerk. I've worked here for ten years. You must've retired quite a while ago."

Her eyes narrowed. "Yes. I suppose."

She turned a saccharine smile to Sarge. "You promised me a nice breakfast this morning."

"Well, I don't like to keep a lady waiting." He offered the vile woman his arm.

Nodding to me, he said, "I'll be in touch."

I sighed in relief when they left and began my research.

Shortly before my shift ended, Sarge knocked on my office door. "Can I come in?"

"Sure." I cleared my throat. "I have your numbers. Since 1975, there've been twenty people die by poisoning or mysterious circumstances. Interestingly, they were all members of the same gardening club."

"Which one?"

"Cedar Junction Garden Club. I checked their website. They currently have twenty members, four of whom are founding members. After being active in the same group for such a long time, there's bound to be some tension."

"Aunt Sue used to be president of that group," he said. "I'll ask her if there's anyone who is prone to bickering. How'd you make the connection?"

"Obituaries." I grinned. "Each of them mentioned the club."

"I appreciate your hard work. How about I take you to dinner, so we can discuss this further?" he asked.

My stomach growled at the mention of food. "Sounds good."

"Great. I'm working a couple hours to fill a staffing gap. Pick you up at seven?"

"Sure. Do you know where I live?"

He grinned. "In this small town? I'll find you."

"Okay," I said. "See you then."

Studying my closet, I wondered what someone wore to an off the clock working dinner. Definitely not what I'd wear on a date. I decided to keep it casual with a pair of linen slacks and loose-fitting blouse.

Sarge knocked on my door at seven sharp.

"Hi," I said.

"Ready to go?"

I nodded. Grabbing my purse, I stepped outside into the furnace we call Missouri in August. "Where are we going?"

"Is pizza okay with you? I'm in the mood for something cheesy."

I gave him a genuine smile. "I love pizza. Sam's or Louie's?"

"Louie's," he said with a nod. "They have the best sauce."

Secluded in the back booth of our local pizzeria, I

withdrew a pen and paper from my purse to make notes. "All of the victims seem to have lived fairly close to each other."

"I noticed that, too. I have a few of the crime scenes marked on a map at home. Want to see it and help me mark the new locations?" he asked.

"It might help put things in perspective."

As soon as I entered his house, Sue glared at me from the couch. "Grace, is it?"

I smiled. "Nice to see you again, Sue."

She flattened her lips. "I wasn't expecting to see you at all. Certainly not here with my nephew."

"Grace is helping me with a case." He turned to me. "Aunt Sue is staying with me while she's visiting the area."

"I sold my house when I moved to Florida last year after my husband died," she said. "I'm a fun-in-the-sun kind of woman."

I smiled, forcing myself to be friendly. "That sounds lovely. How long will you be visiting?"

"I'm spending six weeks here. Even though I love Florida, I did get a little homesick. I think I'll be ready to head back next week."

"You're welcome to stay as long as you like," Sarge said. "It's getting late, so we better get busy. We'll be in the study."

Entering the sparsely furnished space, I was startled when something rubbed against my leg. "Oh!" I looked down to find a beautiful tabby cat. "Who's this?"

Sarge grinned. "Missy, my best buddy."

Missy circled my legs as I added colored pushpins to the map.

"They're all in the center of town," I said. "Very close to the garden club."

"Interesting. Let's go talk to Aunt Sue," he said. "She'll know if there were any rifts within the membership."

We joined the older woman in the living room where

she was watching TV. "Aunt Sue, we'd like to ask you about the local garden club."

She eyed me suspiciously. "What about it?"

"Was there ever any bad blood, feuding, or anything amongst the members?" he asked.

"No more than any other club. Why?"

"Just curious," Sarge said. "Can you remember anyone who was particularly hostile to anyone else? Any scandals?"

"Well, Randy and Thelma had an affair that came to light after Randy's wife saw them walk into the Kitty Cat Motel together. That was pretty scandalous. They both got divorced. Randy left town, and Thelma died of a heart attack before the dust settled."

I searched my memory. "Would that be Thelma Jones?"

Sue looked surprised. "Yes. That all happened years ago. How do you know her last name?"

I looked Sarge in the eye. "Hers was one of the suspicious deaths I marked."

Sue stood, her eyes developing a crazed gleam. "How about a nightcap?"

My spine tingled. "No thanks."

"Sure," Sarge replied.

Sue marched into the kitchen and returned with three cocktails a few minutes later. "I know you said you didn't want one, Grace, but it's my special recipe. You really must try it."

I raised my glass, sniffing. There was a faint whang of something that didn't belong. I'd always had a keen sense of smell and had learned to trust my nose. As Sarge raised his glass to his lips, I panicked and knocked it from his hand.

Liquid pooled on the floor where Missy was quick to sniff it. Recoiling with a hiss, her hackles rose.

"They're poisoned," I said.

"Nonsense!" Sue shouted. "That dumb cat is

overreacting."

Sarge walked to the closet, grabbing his tactical bag as his aunt sputtered. He poured my drink into an evidence vial. "We'll see."

As they argued, I went to the kitchen, examining every surface. I found green powder on a cutting board where something had been crushed. Opening a Cool Whip container, I gasped.

"Sarge, you need to see this," I hollered.

He stomped into the kitchen, a firm grasp on his aunt's upper arm.

I showed him the contents of the container. "Green Eastern Black Nightshade berries. Highly toxic."

"No. I would never." Sue looked up at Sarge and changed her story at his dark expression. "You don't understand. They were all out to get me, just like your uncle. They had to go. It was them or me."

Bile rose in my throat. "How many people have you murdered?" I asked.

Glaring at me, she snarled, "Apparently, one less than I should have."

A Lethal Taste

A Haiku

Daphne's sweet cookies
Angie's bite, a lethal taste
Whispers of murder

FIXATED

Sarah's thoughts raced as she shivered in the early December sleet and wind. Wanting nothing more than to go home and crawl into bed, she'd been frantically working on a presentation all day and half the night.

She fumbled for her keys as she drew near her car. The sound of footsteps startled her, and she spun around to peer behind her. The sidewalk and street were deserted, but her skin itched like someone was watching her.

Clutching her keys, she hurried to her car. She clicked the keyless entry as soon as she was within range. She paused long enough to open her door and slide into the driver's seat, locking herself inside.

Air rushed in and out of her lungs as Sarah took a careful look around. Again, she saw nothing. The sidewalk and street were deserted. Sleet fell steadily, freezing on her windshield as her heart pounded.

Shaking her head at her own foolishness, she started the car and hit her defroster button. A quick glance in the rearview mirror revealed her brown eyes were red from the cold wind, and frost was clinging to her dark hair and eyelashes.

She was rubbing her hands together when she noticed a note sealed in a zipper bag under her wiper blade. With another careful look around, she opened her door, grabbed the note, and locked herself back inside.

I'm watching you. I like your hair up like that. It shows off your milky white throat that will soon bear my mark. I am always watching you.

Sarah was completely paralyzed with fear as she waited for her defrosters to do their job. Once she could see through her windows, she put the car in gear. Racing through the streets at a breakneck speed, she told herself she had nothing to fear, but she couldn't quite make her hands stop shaking or her heartbeat return to normal.

When she arrived home, she opened the garage door with her remote and inched her car inside before cutting the engine and hitting the remote to close the door. She sat in the silence of her garage for a few minutes before opening her door and climbing out.

Trudging to the connecting door between her garage and kitchen, she flicked on the light, kicked off her boots with a sigh, and padded to her bedroom. She switched on her bedside lamp, dropped her purse and keys on the nightstand, and began to undress.

As she slipped out of her slacks, she glanced over to her bed and froze. There on her pillow was another note. Her heart raced once more, but the fear was quickly replaced by seething anger.

Not thinking logically, she snatched the note and opened it.

I'm still watching you. You look delicious tonight. I will come for you soon, and then we'll play. I'm going to show you what happens to pretty girls who think they're better than everyone else.

Sarah stomped through the house to the living room where she kept her old-fashioned landline phone. She never had to worry about dropped calls with that one, so she kept it. After hastily dialing twice to no avail, she realized her phone line was dead.

Panic gripped her with icy fingers. Bolting back to her bedroom, she frantically searched through her purse for her cell phone. She always kept it in her purse, but it was missing. As she reached for the keys she'd tossed on the nightstand, she realized she wasn't wearing any pants.

Snatching her dirty pants from her bedroom floor, Sarah slipped them on and ran for the garage.

As she reached the connecting door, all the lights went out. She was so startled by the sudden darkness that she dropped her keys. She sank to her hands and knees to feel around for them and heard something behind her. She looked up as someone very large and strong grabbed her with a hand over her mouth and an arm around her waist, lifting her into the air. She wriggled, kicked, and tried to hit. The person holding her seemed to have arms of steel.

"I told you I would come for you," said a deep male voice. "I've been watching you for weeks, and now we're going to play!"

Sarah fought harder, desperation nearly suffocating her, until her attacker punched her across the face with such brutal force that darkness claimed her. When she regained her faculties, her wrists were bound with duct tape, her right eye was throbbing, and she was in total darkness. She could hear the man shuffling around in the bedroom. He rummaged through her things for a bit and then started back towards her. She could hear every footstep, even though she could not see a thing.

"Ah," came the man's voice from the darkness. "I see you're awake."

She turned her head toward his voice to try to discern his precise location. She could make out the outline of a very large man as her eyes adjusted.

"What do you want with me?" she asked.

His high-pitched maniacal laughter echoed through her kitchen. He stared at her for several moments before reaching out and grabbing her by her hair. He yanked her head back, and she could feel his putrid breath on her face.

"I've been watching you and thinking how much fun it

would be to play with you. You all but invited me to make myself a key when you left your purse in your office unattended. You never even knew I was there because I was so stealthy." He chuckled. "I know you want to play. I can tell by the way you're always moving your shoulders around and tossing your hair, just begging for a man to give you what you deserve."

"So, I work with you? Who are you? How can we play a game if I'm tied up? It wouldn't be a fair game at all," Sarah said frantically.

"You being tied up is all part of the fun," he said. Tightening his hold on her hair, he licked her throat from her collarbone to her jaw. His breath, a noxious cloud of whiskey and garlic, coated her skin in a foul mist.

"You have a nice little place here. The houses are a good distance apart. Your closest neighbors are all old and hard of hearing. It's perfect. No one will interrupt our fun." His tongue traced her ear as his fist pulled her hair harder.

Sarah's life flashed before her eyes, all her regrets surfacing to taunt her. She'd been married to her job and made no time for friends or family. No one would even miss her until Monday.

"What do you want to play?" Sarah asked between dry lips.

"There are so many fun games I want to play with you," he answered. "I think we should start with Burning Girl. That's where I heat up one of my toys and then see how long I can hold it to your skin before you faint again. It's one of my favorite games."

The man abruptly released her hair, and she heard him walk into the living room and rummage around. When he returned, she caught a quick glint of silver and noticed he was wearing night vision goggles as he passed by her kitchen window. He turned on the stove and placed the silver object she assumed to be a metal poker of some kind directly on the burner. He was completely engrossed in his task.

Sarah searched frantically for any means of escape. Now that her eyes had adjusted to the darkness, she could make out a few shapes. She noticed her boots still sitting beside the connecting door. They were only a couple feet away from her chair. She quietly extended one leg and slumped down in the chair to give herself a little more reach. She could almost touch the top of one of the boots with her foot. She only needed a couple more inches.

Heaven seemed to smile upon her in that moment because her captor began to hum loudly to himself. She scooted the chair as quietly as she could toward her boots. It felt like hours, but she finally managed to get close enough to slip her foot inside one of them, and then did the same with the other.

She said a silent prayer she would live through this and promised herself she would make some serious life changes. Taking a few deep breaths, she prepared herself for what she was about to attempt.

Her captor returned, holding the glowing red metal object. As he neared her, she kicked out with her booted foot and caught the man in the solar plexus with a vicious kick. The metal object dropped to the floor, and Sarah kicked the man again, this time in the groin. He grunted and lunged for her, but she flung her chair back out of his reach, kicking him in the throat with the sharp heel of her boot. He fell to his knees gasping for breath.

Maneuvering the chair to her silverware drawer, she managed to open it. She grasped a steak knife with her fingers and cut through the duct tape binding her wrists.

Leaping to her feet, she ran for the door. She could hear her captor still gasping for breath on the floor. When he saw her run, he struggled to his feet and attempted to give chase.

She ran toward her neighbor's house and had almost reached his back door when her tormentor caught up and tackled her to the frozen ground. She landed on her back hard enough to see stars.

Sarah screamed, "Somebody help me! Call the police!" as they rolled around on the ground.

The attacker punched her in the ribs and wrapped his hands around her throat, squeezing viciously. Just as she feared she would die on Mr. Simpson's lawn, she spotted a snow shovel leaning against a storage shed not far away.

Sarah punched her attacker in the nose while simultaneously bringing her knee up to his groin. While the man was caught off guard, she shoved him off her. Dashing to the shed, she grabbed the snow shovel and spun around to face the person so determined to seriously hurt or kill her. He was already up and rushing her.

She swung the shovel in an upward arc, catching him in the face. He reeled backward, and she hit him in the midsection before he could regain his balance. As he doubled over in pain, she brought the shovel down on his foot with all her might. Then she slammed it down on his head with a force that would have done John Henry proud.

Satisfied her attacker was finally down for a while, Sarah stumbled toward the house just as Mr. Simpson opened the door and flipped on the porch light.

"I called the police," Mr. Simpson said. "Sarah Rains? Is that you? Are you all right? What in the world happened?"

Sarah fought to catch her breath. "This guy broke into my house, tied me up, and tried to hurt me."

Mr. Simpson's eyes narrowed. "Did he now? You go on in the house and warm up. I'll make sure this creep doesn't go anywhere."

Sarah looked down then and was shocked to see Mr. Simpson was holding a shotgun. His hands were steady on the gun, his gaze sharp.

"We need more light, Mr. Simpson. I need to see the face of the man responsible for this nightmare, and the porch light doesn't reach that far."

"There's a flashlight in the kitchen."

Sarah grabbed the flashlight from the house and shined the beam on her attacker's face.

"Tom!" Sarah yelled. "What the hell? Why did you try to hurt me? What did I ever do to you?"

"How do you know this guy?" Mr. Simpson asked.

"He's the janitor from my office building. I don't know him that well, but I've always been nice to him."

Tom's greasy blond hair hung in strings around his bloody head, his beady brown eyes glaring up at her. His lips formed a sneer, but he refused to speak.

Sarah shook with outrage, but she resisted the urge to kick the man while he bled all over Mr. Simpson's lawn.

"There's a cell phone on the ground over here. Is it yours?" Mr. Simpson motioned to a phone in the snow.

She walked over to where her neighbor stood. "Yes. That's my phone. He stole it from me earlier today and must've dropped it while we fought."

The police and an ambulance arrived and transported Tom to the hospital with an armed escort. An officer took Sarah's statement and promised to be in touch if Tom said anything.

She walked carefully home that night and made certain all her doors and windows were locked. The officer called and explained that after a brief interrogation, her tormentor had confessed to everything. Tom had become fixated on her during her late working hours and followed her home on multiple occasions until he knew her routine.

While she was still processing what the officer told her, he continued. "You aren't his first victim. He confessed to attacking four other women, none of whom survived to tell the tale. You stopped a serial killer tonight. You're lucky to be alive."

"Thank you for letting me know," Sarah murmured into the phone. "I am grateful to have survived."

"I'm sure the prosecutor will be calling you in the next

few days. She'll want to interview you, and you'll probably need to testify. In the meantime, try to get some rest."

When she finally glanced at the clock, it was just after midnight. She lay in bed unable to sleep. Mr. Simpson had changed her door locks while she talked to the police, but it did little to soothe her.

Rolling out of bed, she settled at her desk and opened her laptop. A few minutes later, she had found that which she sought. Kickboxing classes were held every Saturday. She would be first in line for the beginner's session.

ART WILLIAM L. BREACH

Art William L. Breach is a native West Texan who worked for the City of El Paso as a staff writer on numerous regional publications. While grounded in nonfiction, he embarks on journeys as a dark fantasist through stygian gulfs where black planets roll without aim in their horror unheeded, without knowledge, or lustre, or name.

The Daggers of Lament

Fall was heavy upon my brow when the old, familiar footsteps of Memory resounded upon my cobbled walkway. Their somber, unmistakable rhythm beckoned me to dance to their ever-changing cadence. *Depart hence,* I thought; the fatigue of years had wrested from me the youthful prance I had once known. I no longer gaily swayed to Life's rhythms. I sat in contemplation gazing at the dying embers in the hearth.

Wispy tendrils of blissful slumber playfully caressed and tugged at the fringes of consciousness. Oft times I took refuge in their proffered embrace with beloved shards of yesteryear as giftings.

On wings of gentle dreams, I wafted to ethereal shores where bloom alluring, iridescent, narcotic lotus blossoms too beautiful to have been seeded in the cold greyness of this drab, waking world.

This day differed. Slumber fled at the intense, persistent rapping of this trespasser's summons upon my door. Reluctance held me fast. An ominous quality bereft of dearness chilled the fabric of my being. Intuitively, the time for all dreams had come to an end. Inwardly I mourned at the passing of joyful slumber. Never again would I feel its embrace.

Despair and the solitude of years awaited on the other side of that thin boundary separating me from eternity. The door creaked open to something familiar. Sardonically I smiled. Memory nodded. Rustling leaves in autumn's array of colors eddied in strange patterns across the well-manicured yard that once bore the playful longings of a hopeful child.

I glanced furtively behind me. My small, faithful companion of years looked up. Her soft brown eyes gazed quizzically at me. Her brushed tail wagged with enthusiasm in anticipation.

A journey to somewhere, Daddy?

Yes, my little one.

A gentle hand on my shoulder drew my attention forward. *Bid her attend you one last time.*

"Bearly! Come to Daddy!"

She sprang to life prancing in her own inimitable way and came to my side.

A refreshing breeze gently caressed me as we stepped into a festive bygone time. Flowers bloomed. Birdsongs filled the air. Opalescent balloons bobbed to thermals as they waltzed majestically across the skyline to an unheard symphony known exclusively to them.

My white picket fence in newness with its arching entrance gaily gleamed in the sunlight. The scars of time and weather were no longer apparent upon their posts. They stood resolute. A welcome to all travelers.

We passed through this sturdy, wooden gate with its arching posts. I stopped and gazed mournfully at our little homestead with its shuttered windows and solid exterior that weathered so many a storm. Tears brimmed my eyes. Melancholy gripped me despite the ethereal splendor of that day long ago. Tugging at my sleeve indicated the urgency of the hour. With a remorseful sigh of resignation, I conceded with a dispirited nod.

The road before us was long but filled with adventure. The lush overhang of trees along the gently curving path provided a canopy of comfort in soft varied greens. Ethereal lilting flute music, from origins unknown, surrounded us. For a brief moment upon that road, mirth danced in Bearly's eyes and surely reflected in my own.

The inexorable, relentless march of time carried us forward. Balloons in abundance once filling the heavens had altogether disappeared. The former lush canopy thinned; branches drooped. Rustling in the shrubbery drew my attention. A maiden most fair stepped out to greet us. Her alluring smile and pleasant demeanor charmed me. I stopped for a moment. Our unremembered dialogue was all too brief.

We moved on.

Soon thereafter Bearly stopped and rested on the path. Looking up, her aged eyes lost their mirth. Only a bleared shadow remained to indicate it had once been there. She stood and walked into the shrubbery lining the curving path on either side. I called out after her. She turned, wagged her tail, and disappeared into that dense, forested vegetation. My attempt to pursue her was arrested. I lingered, not wanting to continue the journey. From the protective covering denied me, she stared. Our gaze entwined. The twinkle in her eyes returned as did her youthful golden, shimmering coat. She gave a playful bark one last time and was gone.

At the road's end, you will understand.

The sun moved swiftly across the skyline on its descent. In silence three small children, varying in age, stepped out from the hedgerow. They exuded an eerie, alien quality unnerving in familiarity. Their lifeless, expressionless faces with blank stares horrified me. I wanted no part of them. Sensing my apprehension, they returned from whence they came in nonexistent silence.

I hastened my pace. Fragments, shards of my life, things remembered and long forgotten ebbed and flowed in and out of the flanking hedgerow. My life paraded before me in scenes of what was and what might have been. Gay and somber alike each bore the scars of time's cruel whip.

I was overtaken by an awareness my journey had come to an end. I speculated this knowledge, deriving its source from a stooping solitary figure in the distance. Tentatively approaching, I discerned the figure to be a man wizened by time. Downcast eyes bore the burden of a thousand generations. Each disfiguring crease, a wounding slash attesting to Life's cruelty. Torrents of tears lamented numerous lives left in its cascade.

The setting sun, casting him in long shadows, fell deeply.

A cold, grey, pointing finger of accusation tore through me. In disquietude I turned, tracing its finger. In progression each event and the characters of life's play stood staring at me in cold attribution. A gnarled hand on my shoulder drew my attention back.

Deathly stillness ensued. *"Let us finish this journey together."*

The sun lingered briefly over the looming mountains in the distance. Tears afresh cascaded down his weathered features.

"I bear the weight of mankind's remorse upon my shoulders. You've known and walked with me lo these many years. I am Regret."

Sadly, Memory stood smiling before slowly vanishing into the clutching hand of Time. *Now you understand.*

The sun, losing its grip, sank beneath the horizon. With those parting words we faced the road's end together. The daemon of Life, who set me upon this accursed journey, would never again harp to me disquieting songs of remembrance. Together we walked the path's remnant into a cold, dark night.

ELSIE

Only fragments remain. Before I play the final hand I've been dealt, my distraught, haunted spirit demands an ear for what must be done. I have of late, with bitter confession, lost all mirth, forgone all custom of exercise weighing so heavily with my disposition that they now abrade against the insipid pleasantries of the life I once cherished. I convey from necessity what motives, driven by madness, have led me to this. It ends here. But first, you must know why.

I've transgressed the laws of God and nature for a damnable quest. On darkened shores of ignorance, I should've remained. A siren's call from murky, chthonic depths lured me beyond the point of no return. Readily I surrendered in my diminished state of mind Intellectually, I cannot justify my actions; they weren't forged in reason's crucible but in other things, ancient and primordial, fear and affliction.

In the vast array of scientific disciplines and human dynamics, incompatibilities exist whose volatile properties were never meant to be amalgamated. They cannot stabilize within an encumbering, fluctuating emotional framework.

Human ingenuity, coupled with unhindered curiosity, has forged monumental advancements. Knowledge must be tempered by wisdom; not emotions' volatile whims. Monstrosities hence have emerged from it. In depths of affliction, merged with scientific curiosity, I have grievously infringed against humanity.

Summer was brutal. A sweltering heat beat down upon the desert southwest leaving its residents uncomfortably drenched. I often playfully chided my sister, Elsie, that she would have made an exceptional mail carrier who always delivered undeterred. She retorted in her common, lively demeanor that she was always delivering on a hectic schedule – speaking at conferences, setting up for book signings, doing podcasts, crafting her latest literary masterpiece, and the assorted hoops and highwire acts all writers go through.

Although an acclaimed passionate educator, her true zeal lay elsewhere. At an early age she found her passion in writing. The creative juices gushed, nothing could stem the flow. Not even teaching. She retired early to pursue her ardent love.

Years prior, verily to the days of our youth, she traversed many a predecessors' paths in exhilaration of cultivating her own side trail. In close observance, aspiring to be like her, I followed suit. While numerous authors intrigued her, no genre captivated her fancy like mystery and suspense.

I found my creative expression elsewhere. She found thrillers and crime. I found fantasy and the dark places between the stars where nameless planets roll aimlessly.

Diligent years fraught with hardship were rewarded. Fame eventually rested favorably on my sister with all its garish trappings. Life is a cruel taskmaster demanding an exacting price for all its worthless ostentatious trinkets. We've been beguiled into believing the inconsequential has merited worth.

In this frantic and meaningless illusory quest for immortality, the consistent hammering on fate's anvils to pound and shape our desired destiny is vain. A fact discovered late, miles down the long and winding road called "life." 'Tis true, we reap in different seasons than we sow, only to learn the years teach us what the days never knew.

Although separated by miles, we communicated frequently. The call came on a Saturday morning in early May. It began in standard fare with my typical greeting.

"Hey, sweets! How ya doin'?"

Pregnant silence.

"Well, I'll never tell you. That's way too personal," she giggled halfheartedly.

It was a friendly raillery with slight variation we played.

Something was amiss.

"Glad you called. You and Rich headed out to New Mexico for that Mystery Writers' Con?" I probed.

"Well, I've got something to tell you. I was out walking Shadow with Rich. . ." I tensed making my way to the kitchen as my sister related shattering news.

Her, my brother-in-law, along with their dog, were out on their early morning constitutional when she collapsed. Richard frantically got them back home and immediately took her to the hospital. Days passed. Results came back. She had an aggressive brain cancer which spread into her esophagus and then into the lungs. She didn't have long. A year at the most, if fortunate.

My world collapsed. All I could stammer out was a tearful, *"No! No! God, no! It can't be!"*

There was no mistake.

Grief-stricken, we parted company. I sat in shocked disbelief as my life, hopes, and dreams were callously ripped away leaving tormented shards to pass through my fingers as they splashed on the floor in pools of tears.

I did not, could not, would not accept it. Where there's a will there's a way. Frantic thoughts lashed through my mind. Inwardly I screamed as barred and bolted doors to subconscious nether regions tore asunder with tornadic force.

Banished things awoke.

A name shrouded in intrigue whirled before me. A name long since evicted from thought but once studied for his remarkable ground-breaking work while I pursued an undergraduate in archeology. Steeped in esoteric lore, a research explorer whose writings and status are legendary arrested my thinking. Shrouded in mystery, and something of an enigma, this ill-fated, tormented soul left a legacy of darkness for generations to follow.

Neither mystic nor wizard, he was a man of science. A charlatan to many. A new age messiah to others. The very thing that gave him notoriety from numerous excursions into the Antarctic, ironically orchestrated his undoing. Being the chair of the science department didn't faze him. Obsessive work abroad in glacial wastelands became his nemesis. Refrains of discord resounding in forlorn iced ballrooms needled him into a slow death waltz with neurosis.

Incoming reports slowly changed, escalating to alarm. Purported perverse artifacts unearthed from the icy wastes of the Antarctic trickled in. If brought to light, they would shatter reality's framework. Key amongst them were arcane volumes of impossible age. Venerated halls of academia along the east coast reportedly housed these monstrosities under lock and key -- until their disappearance.

Best laid plans often go awry. Fueled by financial panic, word soon leaked from the university funding these explorations that monumental discoveries had been made. Boardroom turmoil ensued. What was found under the ice sheets would never be publicized. Damage control was initiated. Disclosures stated the findings were embellished as a ploy to draw attention to the college for much-needed funding. Conflicting reports ensued, enduring to this day, in academic and private sectors. His name and credibility, though besmirched over this controversy, still carried weight. He was, forsooth, as he boasted, New England.

I won't divulge his name nor those of the eldritch tomes I possess. I *know* the truth. Fools will follow. None must traverse the paths I've taken. The secret dies with me.

Reality's boundaries wavered. I can damnably point to the initiating incident when they blurred. New England's mystique captivated me. I was in Providence meandering through outwardly crumbling, unconventional little shops when confronted by the volumes whose very existence were denied. I stared in disbelief.

Despite their alleged inconceivable age, they were well-preserved and inexpensive. Grimacing, I gingerly held the pair. Curious fingertips glided over their surface. *Unreal! They trembled under my touch!* I fought the urge to cast them away and flee that horrible little store. Deriding laughter echoed.

Secrets muttered. I turned an attentive ear. My heart raced. They knew my name. Mere books these were not. Whatever they were should've remained permanently sealed under the ice. I placed them on a table nearby and entered their domain. *The language! I knew it!* Similar to Aramaic yet vastly different in style structure. As an archaeologist, learning philology benefited me on Fertile Crescent sojourns and now here.

How long I spent perusing their content escapes me. Wheezed spasmatic breathing broke my attention. Annoyed, but grateful for the distraction brought by the wizened figure attending me, I closed the books turning to the stooped shop keeper. Thoughts and questions with accompanying "what if" statements cascaded.

Forcibly I shrugged them off and pondered the clever marketing ploy permitted by his estate. After leaving, undoubtedly, there'd be another set of these deceptively tattered, worm-gnawed, *"one-of-a-kind"* volumes to sell to the next ingenuous tourist.

Subtle restlessness toyed with me. An over fraught imagination labored. Controlled fear lurked behind the proprietor's eyes. Showmanship at its finest. We conversed uncomfortably over the questionable volumes. He avoided eye contact. His raspy choked answers came back with rapid sidelong furtive glances. I thanked him and left *knowing* their well-worn appearance had been fabricated. Something lingered I couldn't shake. Behind that thin, skittish smile, absolute terror hid.

Days later, on the return flight home, vexing thoughts still hounded me.

Poor financial management nearly caused the university's collapse. Those legendary Antarctic Expeditions were a last resort to keep them afloat. Notoriety caused by the scandal elevated the university to legendary status. Competition for entrance was fierce and the wait list to attend – *mindboggling!* Contentious storms turned ferocious. Impressive finds were paraded with fanfare amidst the turmoil hoping to quell the matter. Seasoned press hounds barked ruse. Attention was being diverted from wagging tongues who secretively whispered in darkness. I shuddered. Thoughts of the absurd skirted the edges of consciousness. Fitful rest chained me to hellish nightmares which dragged me away.

In ensuing days, I perused the grimoires' ludicrous depictions of impossible biological frights and marveled as to what they represented. The eccentric New Englander, in lengthier works I researched for my own writing, whose titles elude me, save that "madness" appears in one or two of them, ominously forewarned readers to exercise discernment.

Months lapsed. Sleep patterns altered. Stress, deadlines and commitments; what to leave in, what to leave out, work

– the daily grind of life took their toll.

Bewildered, I studied as time allowed.

Fitful nights plagued me. Nightmare's residuals boiled into the daylight hours. Disquietude of being haunted or *hunted* shadowed me. Tenacious mental cobwebs became problematic. I had to know more.

The underlying premise of the tomes were scientific. Unfamiliar star charts and graphs enticed me. Full comprehension became a hindrance. When certain planetary alignments occurred, in conjunction with asterisms, gates or portals were breached through *precise* gravitational pull allowing these dimensional shamblers free access into various multiverses.

But it wasn't unhindered. An Appointed One; an Overseer, a Guardian who Lurks at the Thresholds has sovereign dominion over what passes through and where they are allowed access. Through the practice of certain rituals and incantations correctly performed, this impartial Watcher at the Gate allows those trapped on the other side access into the dimensions where they are being summoned. This Gate Keeper then opens the portals into those specific realms.

Even the key to the gates of life and death it held.

A shot in the dark came– I snatched it from the turmoil screaming in my head! All or nothing. I refused to let my sister die! Frantically I poured myself into the texts utilizing every scrap of knowledge and training I could to ensure flawless delivery. The sooner the better. No time to waste. Days ticked by. The cruel swinging pendulum threatened to drop its blade with each passing sweep. It's now or never.

I summoned this Keeper and waited with uncertainty, while pondering the philosophical tangent of reality.

With great expectancy I hoped.

Nothing.

Tick-tock. . . tick-tock. . .

Elsie's condition worsened.

Still nothing.

The phone rang. Caller ID said "Elsie" My heart smiled for the first time in ages. I picked up not knowing who to expect since family members on my sister's side had the habit of leaving their phones scattered.

"Hello?"

Static. Silence. More crackling static.

I waited.

A low, distant, agonized, imperceptible trapped wind moaned as if swirling in an abyss from which it sought escape. Perplexed, I strained an eager ear. A dead spot. Previously undetected, mixed in the groaning wind, there emanated a feeble piping sound issuing from what sounded like a flute.

"Hello!"

A few seconds later came the labored response. *"L – liiiaaammmm?"*

"Eh. . . Elsie? – is that you?"

Distant but recognizable.

"Yesssss, it's me-h – I . . . missssed ta-lking with youuuu. Be. . . to-gether. . . soooonn. I. . . love. . . youuuu."

Maybe I screamed. I blocked much of it away after that brief encounter.

Elsie passed away months prior to this call.

Oh, my God! What have I done?!

I raced to those hell-spawned atrocities hysterically searching for clues and answers. The second book held the key. In order to yield desired results, the ritual had to be done at a certain time of year and *only* at the proper designated hour, “when the stars are right.” If not, the results would be disastrous.

In desperation I failed to examine and rationalize. I acted in raw emotion not discernment. Reversing the effects was possible – at a high cost. That thing lurking at the gates had to be appeased. Appeasement came through death. The summoner, ending his life would break the circuit. No conduit. No relay switch to complete the cycle.

I burned the books, their ashes divided and buried strategically. Where, I will not say. My body won’t be found either. I made certain of it. I’ve dug my own grave, now I shall lie in it. So much of what life teaches is learned in pain. There is truly a season and time to every purpose under heaven. Who can thwart the hand of God? Death cannot be frustrated nor can there ever be a life of meaning devoid of tears.

I sought to save my sister’s life. In attempting, I ripped knowledge from the clutched fists of Erebus where dark secrets should remain forever concealed.

On Wetted Wings They Come

Weighted and loathsome it hung in the night sky on that spectral, fated bygone autumn of madness. Bearing the semblance to a lopsided oyster, the moon's distorted, awkward appearance lent itself to its haunted, ghastly visage. A rolling, blue-hued diaphanous cloud cover thinly masked a baleful wavering gaze teasing a watchful Earth.

Across rolling darkened landscapes, awash in leprous tints, jutting trees textured the Ozarks as diseased, festering pustules rupturing on the earth's surface. Low moaning winds, moving through restless arbors, resonated with indecipherable garbled whispered chants from forbidden depths of deathless iniquity.

A familiar aberrant rhythmic beat pulsated into the night's encumbering shroud. From the front porch of the family cabin, nestled deep in the rolling woods, Jeff Hawley strained a nervous, reluctant ear to the night's unwelcomed encroachment and things brought on the wing. Hesitant mental amorphous appendages plucked at darting sound fragments tormenting his unhinged nerves. An unshakable growing disquietude incrementally festered as nightfall brought appalling distant glimpses of wet, flapping winged horrors riding fetid air currents.

In ruins of smoldering logic, tattered emotions gasped for air while an anguished defiled soul screamed. Trepidation hounded him as a wolf circling its prey. Nights of dread played out virtually unaltered. Day's lapse into dusk ushered in a distressing, palpable element of horror creeping across the horizon carried by whippoorwills in the hills.

Abandoned to the ravages of time and nature, in deep recesses of a primordial forest, crumbled in desuetude a rugged structure once esteemed as a place of high worship. It stood defiant, a testimony in resiliency. Its spires, jutting heavenward at twisted angles tottered, creaking in acknowledgement or accusation to the wind's cadence, the throngs of those whose memories and prayers remained lodged in worm-gnawed walls. Shrill winds screeched hellishly through cobweb-draped corridors once bearing noble splendor. Forgotten edifications bestowed upon rugged pioneers of a bygone era were derided as accursed cries screaming through shadowed corridors. The looming, intimidating presence of Faullen Northfield Church exerted itself sinisterly shadowing the congregants' ruinous graveyard.

Unknown names etched on tombstones whose lives came and went uneventfully littered thc dcad, stagnant earth. Tragic memoirs to arrogant, meaningless, strutting players who fretted their hour upon the stage. All rantings of madmen full of sound and fury bearing significance to a muffled whisper lost in the wind. Reluctantly, his attention was drawn to the unnerving, restless, looming presence vying for his attention. He cursed under his breath.

From childhood's haunted memory, the name Hawley was regarded with antipathy. Scorned and belittled with verbal icepicks, he bore the brunt of generational scorn. Cruel taunts needled his journey into manhood. Laughter and mirth were discarded things of contempt. Though reason and rationality shielded his solitary fortification, he wasn't impervious to chinks in the structure's fabrication despite consistent efforts at the bulwark's maintenance.

Repudiated fear skirted the edges of rationality. Seeds of skepticism watered in doubt germinated in fear's cold soil. The mélange of fact from fancy had to be separated in reality's crucible regardless of where that trajectory lay. The assemblage of sparce, slowly acquired contentious information tortuously crystalized his blood to ice.

With eyes locked on the crumbling structure, rampant thoughts teetered on a macabre carousel pieced together from an array of nightmares.

It beckoned. He moved toward its commanding summons.

Thump-thump. . .

Another worn-down building tottering on the edge of collapse.

Thump-thump, thump-thump. . .

A brisk gust of autumn's wind scraped him.

He shivered. Night encroached. Shadows lengthened. Deathly silence overtook the glen. Unrest cut deep. Persistence prevailed. Hands balled into fists; he stood defiantly in opposition to the menacing structure. Resolution drove him.

Uncertain if the rickety steps would support his weight, tentatively, he tested each protesting weathered floorboard's endurance. He reached the landing. Brisk strides took him past the once ornate double doors leading into the sanctuary. Therein much vied for his attention.

An ominous weight choked the stagnant air. Its oppressive shroud parted. His presence, the only one to have invaded the closely guarded inner sanctum of the desecrated church, stripped every nuance from the well-guarded, intimidating edifice's selfish clutches. Tattered, splintered pews strewn in disarray were discourteously thrown to the sanctuary's right. Grand hymns of a bygone time had filled the place once. No longer as the smashed organ beneath the choir loft testified.

A thing in time's solitude had been disturbed and it took notice. Whatever sanctity that once reposed there had long since departed.

Trained eyes methodically absorbed curves and angles in an array of faded colours and hues, in schemes and textures. Discarded religious objet d'art hung precariously from rotted walls. In darker recess, sagging cobwebs dangled from rafters buckling under time's ruinous abandonment.

A sizable passage bore into earth's fetid clay from the church's interior left him jarred. Splintered wooden floor planks lining the opening's exterior had the markings of being gnawed.

What had the capacity to chew through the floor to generate this tunnel? The probable existence of such a thing defied calculation.

How long did it take to create this burrow?

A trapdoor in the sanctuary was perplexing. Eerily incongruous, it yawned loathsomely before the pulpit. Its dimensions left him befuddled. The orifice was designed for the passage of something large. Nothing in reason's breadth justified its presence. While pondering this, the thinnest sliver of sanity slipped, crumbling into a swirling cataract whose unfathomable depths were uncharted.

An ominous staircase of rough-hewn hastily placed stone led downward to dubitable regions. It glistened in filtered light sparsely entering the desecrated ruin from stained glass windows still oddly intact. Monotonous walls, comprised of cut blocks lined with crumbling mortar, pressed in on either side. Deep scrapes gouged the ancient walls. By what, was unknown. He cocked one ear and then the other. Silence screamed its defiant reply.

A miasma assailed him. He reeled. It emanated from the pit some 30 feet down front. An explosive clap of thunder derailed his train of thought.

Motion. . .

It began as a low-frequency humming accompanied by a slow turning intensifying vibration of seismic activity emanating from the earth's bowels beneath the sanctum.

A sound birthed from the restless silence bellowed from the terrifying aperture. It was not altogether a horse's neighing, nor the cackling laughter of a hyena, nor the screech of a bat, but something accursed. In frenzied circles he whirled in time to the nefarious symphonic strains of intricate madness playing about him. The odorous stench, belching from the unhallowed pit, was amplified by accompanied movement.

The offensive unwholesome sounds along with the sickening turning motion abated. Peace, however, did not ensue. Another sound equally vile and ominous arose from those benighted charnel legions. A thin, whining mockery of a feeble flute assailed his ears setting his teeth on edge. In frantic desperation, he hunched down clasping his hands over his ears while pressing his eyes tightly together attempting to block out every incongruous sight mocking logic's foundation.

It lasted momentarily. He couldn't be caught exposed in such a vulnerable state. In accompaniment to the repellent piping was the sound of strange, thick waters ebbing and flowing sluggishly on sunless shores. Keen hearing pinpointed the origin as emanating from the aperture leading beneath the abominated church.

Disquietingly unhealthy, it lacked the soothing effect of clear, sparkling waters awash on sunny beaches. A mental impression lingered of thickly lapping, slimy oily waters vomiting on pestilential shores. Putrescent juices produced by the rot of innumerable ages left to ferment in earth's cauldrons until they could no longer be contained and spilled out to deep oceans afoul with decay.

In stinking shallows, nameless things splashed sickly in noxious tides. The sounds produced indicated something formidable in stature and large enough to pass through the Tartarian abyss feet away. Forms no sane mind should fathom, or existence contemplate, moved in restless expectancy. Abrupt ominous silence fell.

Shelter! Move – now!

Disarrayed pews offered the best concealment and protection. As a rodent scrambling from a predator, he darted to the hastily discarded pile. His throbbing heart reverberated in his ears. Seconds became hours. The shelter offered a strategic vantage point. Night lay heavy. Driving rain hammered atop the roof. To the left, a stir of motion immediately outside the worship center's entrance drew his attention. A repulsive black cloaked mass moved stiffly as it filled the ruinous church. An eager swarm awaiting instruction, assembled for liturgical ceremony, shuffled before the yawning void. Silence ensued. Their restless impatience escalated. The throng wriggled awkwardly. No sound emanated from them as their tattered habits rubbed against each other. Even the myriad footfalls fell in silence and did not echo in the ancient chamber.

He shivered, for he did not like the things the night brought and wished bitterly that his forefathers had not been a part of this arcane history. He prayed the unholy silence would break, fearing accidental movement might bring the pest gulfs to bear upon him. For the endurance of an eternity, the only discernable sound was that of pelting rain.

In squirming uncontrolled anticipation, they writhed offensively. Their uncanny movement mocked human motion range in angles incongruous to the norm.

A low lilting flute from nether depths brought the congregants to an immediate stand still. One robed figure, positioned towards the front of the beckoning void, awkwardly held up a volume so loathsome Jeff convulsed in horror of it. One of the few known copies in existence in the Americas had been buried with an ancestor who had met their ignominious end so long ago. Photos, tucked in his desk drawer at the family cabin, identified the detestable thing as *The Journal of Aben Schavel*; known to predate the fabled *Necronomicon* vaulted away at the Miskatonic University in Arkham.

One by one the cowled throng sank into the voracious aperture. As the last grotesque one sank into the depths, he fought the innate desire to flee the hellish place. What if scenarios played out endlessly in his frantic mind's depths?

Before he could make a planned strategic retreat, the turning of earth's charnel diabolical region recommenced with such intensity he thought the weakened edifice would finally buckle under its proclamation. The thunderous roar of hooves mounting the unnaturally hewn staircase were accompanied by a bizarre swooshing sound as only wings might make.

A black vomited stream of atrocities exploded from the enormous opening at the pulpit's base unleashing into the night a foul army taken to the wing. With skillful dexterity the congregants rode those winged horrors. The sound emanating from them was well suited to their being. These hybrid winged things no sound mind could grasp or entirely remember were partially equine in structure with chiropteran features.

He sought to close his ears against the cackling, hyenalike sound they made. In haste they flew out the double doors and into the raging storm. An earsplitting whirring of whippoorwills responded in challenge. When he was certain the last of the foul horde had finally left, he ran out in maddening desperation to flee the lunacy consuming his life. Flashes of lightning illuminated the skyline. The winged black horde took notice as he retreated. The pest gulfs rapidly descended upon the unwelcomed intruder. The whippoorwills charged the nefarious horde making their attack difficult. Grateful for the feathered allies, he took advantage and sought shelter in the adjacent woods where he could strategically retreat back up the road to where he had parked.

The birds had advantage and kept the black horsemen locked in battle over the fallen church. The deafening cacophony of the aerial battle sent him screaming into the night as two empires battled for supremacy across the sky.

Jeff Hawley informed his intimate circle of his quest to debunk misconceptions concerning the family lineage and clear the besmirched name. To the consternation of many, he was urged to adhere to the old axiom of letting sleeping bones rest. He refused.

Weeks passed. He was found in the family cabin half crazed. Nothing verbally could be extracted, save for what had been left in a journal detailing the harrowing ordeal. In a quest to uncover truth from penned delusional ramblings, his family set out to untangle the intricate threads woven into the tapestry of his complex mind.

Faullen Northfield Church had burned to the ground some fifty years prior in a violent thunderstorm that passed through the area. As for the cemetery, Missouri's Land Development in the Ozarks had relocated it to another undisclosed district not held in public records.

Regional professors in the geosciences disavowed the existence of any sort of subterranean lakes, much less an ocean existing beneath the Ozarks. The claim was dismissed with a sneer.

Attending physicians and other doctors skilled in the study of psychosis remained perplexed as to the events he described. Biologically, what he put to paper could not possibly exist. Odd manifestations of a nervous collapse.

Admittedly they could not explain nor authenticate some of the strange substances on parts of his tattered clothing despite intense research and testing conducted.

Other unresolved concerns dealt with curious reports of peculiar people the locals were reporting to authorities. They moved in the concealment of shadow having an unnatural air about them in the horrid, stiff, awkward manner in which they moved through the streets in the dead of night. All attempts to stop one of them for questioning proved to be frustratingly elusive.

And then there were reports of distinct odd sounds emanating from deep in the woods. They were described as something akin to laughing hyenas, although not entirely as they merged with the unnatural frequency of a neighing horse, culminating with a nerve-shattering screech, which was quickly followed by whippoorwills in the hills.

Shirley McCann

Shirley McCann is the author of the Amazon best-selling series, The Scarry Inn, as well as other mysteries. Her award-winning short stories have appeared in Woman's World, Alfred Hitchcock Mystery Magazine, and The Forensic Examiner, as well as numerous other publications.

In addition to writing mysteries and short stories, she has also penned two romance novels.

Shirley is a co-founder of Springfield, Missouri writers' group, Sleuths' Ink Mystery Writers. She also maintains memberships in The Springfield Writers' Guild and The Ozark Romance Authors.

A Life of Content

"Helen, did you see the electric bill this month?"

"No, why? Can't you find it?"

"Oh, I found it. And let me tell you, I'm about to explode." Walter waved the bill in the air in front of his wife's face. "Honestly, if this keeps up, we may have to move into a tent."

"Well, that's a ridiculous thought now, isn't it? What would we use for electricity and water? And what about all our electronics?"

Walter glared at his wife. "You think this is all a big joke, don't you?"

Helen pulled the lever on the electric recliner and aimed the remote at the eighty-five-inch television and sighed while she continued to flip through channels. "Well, there's not much we can do about it now, is there?"

Sometimes Walter wondered why he'd married such an airhead. Twenty years was a long time to commit to a woman with only half a brain. The only thing she did all day long was sit in front of the television, surfing channels and stuffing her fat face with junk food.

And if that wasn't bad enough, during the winter months, she bumped the heat up to eighty degrees, while he came home from an exhausting day's work to a scorching house where he could barely breathe.

The summer months were no better. She followed the same routine except the air conditioner was turned down to a freezing sixty degrees, while she sat in her recliner with her fuzzy slippers on her fat feet, a blanket around her and a bag of cookies.

"By the way," she said with a wave of her jiggly arm, "your dinner is in the microwave, so just heat it up and leave me alone to watch my show. *Dancing With the Stars* comes on in a few minutes, and I don't plan to miss it."

Walter gritted his teeth and walked up behind the recliner with his fingers gnarled into a menacing gesture. If he had any guts, he'd end this nightmare of a marriage right now.

Every meal they consumed came from the frozen section of Walmart. Seriously, how hard was it to boil some noodles and add a can of spaghetti sauce? Even a hamburger-helper-type meal would be a treat once in a while.

In the kitchen, he set the timer on the microwave and waited for his macaroni and cheese to heat up. Minutes later he sat at the kitchen table and spooned some of the gaumy concoction into his mouth. A drink of water did nothing to ease the nauseating texture of his meal.

Exhaling a loud gush of air, he tossed his napkin on the table and stood up. Enough was enough.

He stormed across the room and stood next to his useless wife, blocking her view of the television. "Now you listen to me," he said, bending down to wave a finger in her face, "either you start doing some actual work around here, and start using less electricity or I'm gonna have to—"

"What? Kill me?" She kicked at him with her foot, barely missing his jewels. Then she actually had the nerve to laugh. "You do realize cooking with a microwave uses much less electricity than heating up an oven or stove, don't you?" She moved her huge torso to the right to get a better look at the television. "Now get out of my way."

Walter seethed through gritted teeth. How much could one man take? Marriage was supposed to be a fifty-fifty relationship, right?

Blowing a calm stream of air through his lips, he walked away until he stood behind his wife again. With a satisfied smile, he removed the tie from his collar and quickly secured it around his wife's neck. She kicked and clawed until all signs of life drained from her body and she slumped in the chair, while the remote slid to the floor.

After pleading guilty to murder, Walter resigned himself to the fact he would spend the rest of his life in prison for killing his wife.

When the prison transport vehicle delivered him to his new residence, Walter took a moment to gaze at the huge monstrosity he would call home for his remaining years. But the only thought that crossed his mind was how high their electric bill must be. Then he chuckled as his shackled body was led into his new home, realizing it was no longer any concern of his.

DAVID C. REED

David C. Reed is a former criminal investigator who transforms real-world experiences into sharp storytelling that grip from the start as every page cuts deeper. His stories are steeped in authenticity, grit, and the raw choices that define the best and the worst of us.

The Fire Watcher

I can trust you, right? It's been long enough I think, and I left that area over thirty years ago. But still, I don't want people to think I'm crazy. If you'll hear me out, I swear this is absolutely true. But please, don't interrupt or I won't be able to finish.

See, in my hometown of Harmony, cows outnumbered the people five to one. In 1992, I was happily married, a small cattle farmer, and a deputy sheriff. Less than a year later, I was none of that.

In the fall, we usually had a good deal of out-of-town hunters and campers, so the sheriff's department did get busy with a few rowdy deer camps, a DUI or two, and of course, the occasional lost person. But while autumn was still in the air, there was one other big problem we faced.

Wildfires.

Whether it was an untended campfire or a careless cigarette didn't much matter. Wildfires could raze hundreds of acres in just days with any kind of wind to move it. I've seen bad ones burn homes and even kill people. We took fire damn seriously there in the fall.

One such year I helped out by dropping off forest rangers so they could walk to their fire towers. An around-the-clock fire watch was established one windy and unseasonably warm week, as the entire region was considered high risk for fires. The rangers were working twelve hours on and twelve off. I volunteered to pick them up at the ranger station and drive them to a thickly wooded trailhead at the end of a dirt logging road.

I got to know a ranger named Dobbs who was a fisherman like me, so we struck up a friendship. He packed a kit he had assembled with a set of good binos, observation logs, a survival knife, and other stuff. After I dropped him off, he'd say it was a half-hour walk up the trail to the fire tower.

There had been several small fires reported, so I had plenty of opportunities to pick him up both before and after his watch. Coming down, he was eager to get home and get a real meal and some quick sleep before his shift started up again.

Going up, we chatted about fishing or hunting. He was easy to talk to and always seemed interested in what I had to say. Just a good old guy. After the watch was called off, we agreed to get together, introduce the wives, and maybe grab our shotguns and dogs to scare up some fall pheasants.

This arrangement settled into a routine, and I could tell the work was wearing on him. One day I was to pick Dobbs up at the trail head at six p.m. That night he was late.

I idled my patrol car at the trailhead and waited for him in the disappearing light. I didn't know what the holdup was, surely a guy as smart as Dobbs had left the tower while still light. I fidgeted in the car. There had to be some kind of goings on he wanted to discuss with his relief and thus was running a little late. He was always hungry coming off shift, so my wife had fixed him a roast beef sandwich and a thermos of coffee. They sat in the seat beside me as the sun went down.

In another half-hour they were cold.

I used my cruiser's spotlight to illuminate up the trail. Did he have a flashlight in his fire watch kit? I couldn't remember. Be easy to get turned around in the dark woods if you didn't have a light. I started to worry about my new friend. I let out a long blast on my car horn to let him know where I was, then I turned on my overhead blue and red lights. Maybe that would help.

Nothing. It was getting cool quickly. Soon Dobbs was over an hour late.

I decided to get out and walk up the trail a bit myself. I radioed in I was checking on him and locked the car, but left it running with the overhead lights on. I took my flashlight and the thermos, then at the last second, I'm not sure why, I grabbed my Winchester rifle.

I was a little nervous about walking into the dark woods. I had never been up this trail before. I'd only seen it from my cruiser. But the trail was plain enough from the heavy recent foot traffic, so I started up.

And up was right. Once out of sight of my car, it took a sharp turn steeply uphill. Soon, and after only a minute or so of walking, I was out of sight of the cruiser and out of breath. While I could still see the flashing cruiser lights reflecting in the treetops, it was easy to see how anyone could get turned around out there.

I gained a new respect for my buddy, Dobbs. I was breathing hard, and my calves began to complain about the sharp up-angle hiking. I had to grab tree limbs to pull myself up as the trail went lazily back and forth, but always steeply upwards. Sweat ran little trails down my back.

I was only able to follow the trail because of my flashlight. Then I had a bad thought. I couldn't remember when I'd put in new batteries. If it went out, I'd be stuck and have to feel my way back through the pitch blackness.

I got a little angry at myself for being so out of shape and unprepared. Considering my situation and the painful progress I'd made, I knew I'd better see the lights on the tower soon or stop and turn back. I was twenty minutes up the trail when I began to smell the smoke.

That meant bad trouble, and not just for Dobbs. I didn't see the telltale orange to red glow in the sky yet that would signal a large forest fire, but the scent of burning wood, growing stronger, was drifting down from above.

As I rested a second, I leaned against a tree and opened the thermos I'd brought for Dobbs. It was quiet, even for this time of year. Usually you'd hear something, especially if there was a fire. The quiet wasn't natural. It was as if the entire forest was holding its breath.

And of all things, I had the uneasy sense I was being watched. Years of tramping through the outdoors taught me what felt right and what was out of place. It was a feeling you had, and hard to explain. You know what I mean.

But right then, for maybe the first time in my life, I had the uncomfortable feeling it was me. *I* was the thing out of place here, and something was *watching me*. I capped the thermos back and moved upwards along the trail as fast as I could.

As I climbed, the smell got worse. I was debating running back downhill to my car and calling in the fire, but surely the rangers were on it.

Then I saw something reflecting my light on the ground in front of me. I stooped and picked it up. It was a ranger hat. Beside it was a revolver, cylinder open, and empty.

Now I was really scared. "Dobbs!" I yelled. "Dobbs!"

My voice echoed through the otherwise quiet woods. I scanned the area with my light but didn't see anything else. *Keep steady*.

"Dobbs!" I screamed louder this time. The sky began to reflect the tell-tale glow of a wildfire.

Then I heard a man's voice say, "Shut up!"

The sudden voice surprised the tar out of me. "Where are you?" I said.

"Keep quiet! *It'll hear us*!" he said to me.

I located where the voice was coming from, about ten feet away, and swung the light at him. I saw Dobbs under a thick patch of cedars, huddled on the ground.

"Turn the light off," he whispered.

I was moving to where he was and clicked off my

flashlight when it occurred to me what he'd said.

'It' would hear us.

Dobbs was shaking with a knife in his hand, and by the dim orange light of the approaching forest fire, I could see his eyes. Wide, panicked, staring up ahead of us.

Smoke was drifting in the air now. Little embers began to drift by. The fire was coming our way fast.

We were at the bottom of an oval clearing, filled with tall grass and sloping steeply uphill toward more big pines. The fire light from above was brighter, so I figured it must be just over the ridge, maybe a half mile ahead.

I offered Dobbs the thermos and asked, "What are you looking at?"

He slapped my hand away. "Be still!"

He pointed at the top edge of the clearing, just inside the woods, maybe 30 yards away. I stared and tried to match where he was looking, but I couldn't see anything. I looked at him, then again followed his stare uphill.

That's when I saw *it*.

At first I saw nothing but trees, then after a few seconds, something moved. I could make out the outline of an upright figure backlit by the glow from the fire. It was as tall, almost as high as some of the trees beside it.

As if it knew where we were, it turned slightly towards us. That's when I got a better look. I could make out only a few facial features, but I could see it had large eyes that were reflecting the dim firelight. I'd seen a hundred bears in my life and let me tell you with absolute certainty.

This was no damn bear.

As I looked at it, it would look at us, then turn to watch the fire behind it. Its face looked almost *human*. It was watching the fire, then us again, as if *deciding what to do*.

As if hearing my thoughts, it suddenly crouched down and picked at the ground nearest it. I noticed its arms were thick and long. Almost knee length. It scooped up some grass to smell, then again looked directly where we were.

Dobbs pointed at my Winchester. I shook my head and pointed at his empty revolver. Maybe I should have shot it then, but I didn't.

I couldn't take my eyes off it as it crouched there, seemingly looking us over. In a couple of minutes, it stood and walked backward into the woods.

You tell me, what animal walks backward? *Upright*?

"Are you okay?" I asked Dobbs. But before he could answer, we heard a loud noise that sounded like "Hoo-off!" Like a giant exhale from the far-right side of the clearing. It was circling the clearing toward us.

"C'mon, Dobbs! Let's go!"

"It was there. I don't know…I shot at it!"

"Where is your relief?" One look at Dobbs once he stood in the growing fire light told me he was going into shock.

"We'll get help, come on."

We started back down the trail, trying not to use the flashlight. Within a few minutes, Dobbs turned to me as we walked.

"I smelled the smoke. Saw the fire over the ridge. There was all types of wildlife running downhill past me, getting the hell out of Dodge."

"Yeah, keep moving, buddy," I said.

"That's when I saw it. It was walking downhill and crossed the trail ahead of me. I think it was flushed out by the fire, too. Once it saw me, oh God!"

Dobbs tried to sit down, but I held him up and made him keep moving with an arm under his.

I heard some brush crashing and limbs snapping off to our left. I told myself it had to be more wildlife running from the fire, but I wasn't about to go look.

"It came at me! I mean straight at me! It *charged*, yelling and raising its arms! I shot at it, I had to have hit it, but it grabbed my bag off the ground and flung it away!"

"My lord," I said.

"You tell me! What does that?"

Dobbs began to shake and suddenly I felt his weight give way. I tried to get him back on his feet, but he'd fainted. I set him down a second to catch my own breath.

Then I heard a loud commotion on our left again, followed by a yell.

I mean a yell like an air raid siren had gone off! You could *feel* it in your ribs, like it went right through you. I had my rifle up, but I was trembling as bad as Dobbs.

I roughly shook him. "Wake up! Dammit, come on!"

When I turned back toward where I'd heard the noises, from high overhead in the treetops, I heard limbs snapping and brush breaking. A rock the size of a foot stool came crashing down beside us.

It was more of a small boulder than a big rock, and it hit a tree and smashed to the ground only a few feet away. Dobbs woke up and screamed.

The rock, a hundred-fifty pounds maybe, had obviously been *flung* at us. I drew in a breath and got mad. I was mad for what this thing was doing to my friend, and mad at it for making me afraid.

Adrenaline? Maybe, but I swung my Winchester around and fired where I thought it had to be hiding. Three shots I levered at it, and after the third I heard it scream. That impossibly loud siren yell again, but this time there was a different note in it. Pain, maybe.

I got Dobbs up. We heard it moving again, parallel to us and off to our left. But a little further off than before.

We heard it yell one more time, from a long way off. But what scared us more? On the other side of the trail, to our right, we heard something *answer* it. That same incredibly loud yell.

There were two of them.

We ran. Shortly, we didn't hear it at all anymore and several firefighting rangers in gear charged up the hill toward us. I could have kissed every one of them.

They took charge of Dobbs, but not before he and I exchanged a look. Without saying anything, I knew we weren't going to tell anyone about what we'd seen.

And until now, I never have. Dobbs quit the service, and I've never seen him since. What happened that night has always kind of eaten at me. I guess it sounds stupid now, huh?

I mean, things like this. You've heard my story, so what do you think?

The Perfect Alibi

A small man with a nervous tick in his face entered the outer office of Matthew Books. Books could see him through his glass door as he stood waiting in front of what used to be his secretary's desk. Books smiled to himself and let him stand there a minute as he refilled his coffee from the pot in his office, then opened his door.

"Sorry. There's no receptionist, buddy."

"Oh. You're… you're Mister Books," he said with a quiver in his words.

Books raised his eyebrows. "Look at you! And they say *I'm* the private investigator. Come in. Coffee?"

The man shook his head and walked straight to a client chair. Just to be funny, Books leaned out into the empty outer office and said, "Hold my calls."

Books noted the man didn't seem amused, but he did note two other things about his visitor. First, he had recently been in the hospital, as indicated by the plastic identification wrist band and several small bandages on his left arm. Then there were the cheap cotton pants and plastic slide on shoes he was wearing.

So secondly, he'd been in jail.

Books sipped his coffee and pointed at the man's clothes and arm. "It must have been a wild night. Tell me, what you need from me?"

"I just got released after three days of questioning down

at Metro Police Headquarters. They gave me these things to wear. I was in the hospital for a week before that and the ambulance cut my clothes off."

"Ah, been getting the treatment from Ten G Park, huh? What were they sweating you for?"

"Murder. They say I strangled the girl in the apartment beside me."

Books nodded sympathetically and pulled open a desk drawer, the one with the tape recorder and the loaded Glock nine millimeter. "Maybe you should start with your name, son."

"Pollock," he said. "It's been on the news."

"Yeah? You have an attorney I hope."

Pollock held up a card to the public defender's office. "Not yet. First, I need someone to help me prove I didn't do this, and more importantly, catch the guy who did."

Seeing the PD's card told Books this was not going to be a lucrative job, so he said, "Hey, your lawyer will need to hear anything you have to say, so why say it twice? Why don't you head over there and—"

"I didn't kill her. The homicide lieutenant didn't believe me. A lawyer, especially a free one, won't either. I need someone to help me prove it."

Books saw that Pollock's tick wasn't just a facial thing. The little man seemed to be jerking and having small spasms all over. Like he was about to leap out of his skin.

Junkie.

"Well, I'm impressed. You rated the homicide lieutenant for questioning. Ol' Pat Keagan wasn't too rough on you, I hope."

"I didn't kill her. I guess I have what you might call the perfect alibi."

"Mr. Pollock, I'm not a public servant, and despite my current lack of administrative support, I'm fairly expensive. Any money you have would be better spent on legal counsel."

"I was dead at the time," he said.

"I beg your pardon?"

"While Jessica was being raped and strangled, I was dead. But I saw the whole thing."

Books slid the tape recorder out and turned it on. "Maybe you should start over and from the beginning."

Pollock slid around some in the chair and looked as if he might start to cry but then shook his head and shouted as if to himself, "I have to stay, I have to stay!"

"Okay. Um, Mr. Pollock, the, ah, murder?"

Pollock punched his fist into his thigh a few times as he twisted his face into a grimace, then drew in a deep breath.

"I'm okay now. I can talk."

Books wasn't too nervous. Pollock looked to be only 5'4 or so and weighed less than the chair he sat in. Books closed the drawer with the pistol.

"I live over on Lindner Street in the Hillview apartments, third floor. Jessica was new in town and had just moved in beside me," Pollock said.

"Yeah, I know the neighborhood."

"Then you know my life was all to crap and that crummy place was all I could afford. Jessica had an excuse. She was new and saving up for a better place. I was… I was on my way out, man."

"Go on."

"I won't bore you with the details, ask Lt. Keagan, but I made up my mind to just, check out. You know, see what was on the other side, I guess. Everybody was done with me anyway, so I stole a hit of Wild White from this guy I knew. Enough to… well, you get the idea."

"This guy you got the drugs from; did *he* kill Jessica?"

"No! Listen. I shot up the stuff and laid down on my bed to just let it all go. But then something weird happened. It felt like I had been there a while, a long while, then I sat up. I figured I must have stolen some counterfeit or something until I turned around."

Books waited, then gestured with his open palm for Pollock to continue.

"I was on the bed. But I was also standing there, looking down at myself still lying on the bed at the same time."

"Ah," was all Books could think to say. He scooted the recorder a little closer. He wanted to get this.

"It's crazy, but I felt so good. So clear! I felt better than I'd ever felt before. I tried to say something, to yell at my old self, but I couldn't. I felt bad for myself, laying there. I was such a mess. I looked around and I could see colors I'd never seen. I could hear the electricity in the wires and smell the water in the pipes. It was amazing!"

Books ignored all this. The kid had obviously been high. "You say you saw this Jessica murdered?"

"Wait! I just looked at my old self. Laying there, so broken. What a waste! I knew right then I had wasted my life and abused the wonderful privilege of life. But then, well, that's when the weird stuff started."

"Oh, so there's a 'weird' part, huh?"

Pollock leaned forward, smiling. "I felt myself being *pulled* away. Up, through the ceiling."

"To… heaven?"

"No, just above the wires and the pipes. I could see through everything perfectly, and even down into my apartment, and hers."

"Jessica's."

"Yeah, she'd just got home and had a guy with her. I don't know who he was, but I described him to Lt. Keagan, even his clothes. I think she liked him at first. She was being all flirty and looked a little drunk. I could hear her heart beating faster. But things turned pretty damn dark, pretty fast."

Books started making notes. "How was he dressed? What did he look like?"

Pollock flopped back in his chair. "I told Keagan all this. She had on a white tank top dress with a little wine stain and red panties. She'd taken off her bra before, because it was stuffed in her purse."

Books stopped writing. "How could you know… ah, yeah. You were floating around dead."

"Anyway, they started making out, but the dude got too rough. He was grabbing her privates and kissing her on the neck too hard. She yelled and slapped him, but he picked her up and threw her to the floor, hard. She must have had the air knocked out of her, because she really didn't move much after that. The guy climbed on top of her, grabbed her neck with both hands, then he… he raped her."

"You saw all this, Pollock. You watched this happen, did you?"

"I reached out and tried to stop him, but when I saw my arm, all weird glowing colors, and no fingers or anything. I found out I couldn't *touch* anything."

"This guy, this killer, did he look like anyone you know? Maybe even a little like… yourself?"

"No, he was taller and blond," Pollock said.

Books realized Pollock hadn't picked up on his insinuation.

"And yet, here you are. All alive and fine and everything."

"I heard a hard pounding, like on my door from behind me. Then I felt myself being tossed around, carried. I felt that tugging sensation again. Everything went white, then dark, then bright again. I woke up in the hospital."

"Any decent brand of Irish whiskey can cause all this, you know."

Pollock didn't seem to hear Books' remark. "The doctor said I was DOA in the ER. I was dead for over twenty minutes. The guy I stole the hit of Apache from, he'd come to kick my ass but saved me instead."

"And Lt. Keagan. I'll just bet he really loved this story."

"No, he laughed at me like you are. Said I couldn't possibly have known about the key under the bed."

"What's that?"

"The killer, his keys came out of his pocket while he was, doing that to her. A key fell off the ring and bounced under her bed. There were some dirty clothes under there. The key was under a pair of blue jeans."

"How did you know…"

"He got up, picked up his clothes and washed himself off in her bathroom sink. Used a towel on himself, too. Then he latched the door chain from the inside and left by the fire escape."

"Okay, Pollock, now you listen to me. I was a cop once years ago, and even in this job I hear all kinds of crazy stuff. But with that kind of story and that kind of detail, why the hell did Lt. Keagan let you go?"

"He didn't. Not for three days. But I overheard something about clothing fibers and DNA. Anyway, the ER doc told them there was no way I could have committed that kind of violent crime as full of the stuff as I was. Thank God for Narcan, huh?"

"So, you're clear of the rape and homicide now. What do you need me for?"

"Not exactly, Mr. Books. Keagan still thinks I was an accomplice or something. And…"

"And?"

"I need you to help me find the, *hey*!"

"Hey? What?"

"Man! This is important! Tell your friend Keagan they got him. The guy they've got stopped out on 31st Street, right now, that's him! I… guess I don't need you after all."

Books tried hard not to roll his eyes. "Look son, come on, I'm not an idiot."

"Wow. It's nice. I mean, really beautiful," Pollock said, and began to twitch again.

Then he collapsed and fell out of his chair to the floor. Books ran around the desk to check on him, but it didn't take a coroner to see.

Pollock had literally dropped dead.

In less than an hour the coroner's people were rolling the body of Pollock out of Books' office. Lt. Pat Keagan was helping himself to some of Books' coffee.

"And that's all he told you, eh?" Keagan said.

Books shrugged. "First time I've ever heard the, 'I was a ghost' alibi."

Keagan took a long sip of coffee, then slammed the mug down. "Well, gotta go, Booksy. Stay away from keyholes."

"Oh no, Pat. Nuh-uh."

Keagan looked at Books for a beat, then closed the office door. "All right. Off the record?"

"What record? Give."

"Kid knew too much. He had to be in the room. That bra in her purse? Dead on. He described the girl's underwear and everything."

"So, you held him, capitol crime, seventy-two-hour rule."

"He was a suicidal junkie. How hard could he be to crack? I figured in eight hours he'd be hard up again and talk, but no! Stuck to his story. When the DNA came in, there was nothing to tie him to that room. I mean, I couldn't prove he'd ever even *walked* into it. Had to spring him for the murder. Oh, we charged him with the drugs we found in his place, but that was only so we could keep tabs on him."

"I guessed that when he said he saw the murder while floating around, that was just a way of admitting he'd done it but couldn't face it. I'm sure there's a shrink term."

"Disassociation, depersonalization, something like that. Yeah, I had the same thoughts."

"But?"

"But… and if this gets out, I'll stand on your darn toes and deny it to your face, Booksy! But he was right what he told you."

"About?"

"About the guy a patrol stopped on 31st. They thought

he looked familiar, like we had a parole violation on him. We didn't, but the blond guy just blurted it out. He told the uniform, 'I killed that girl', just like that."

"Just like that."

"And another thing. The key we found under the bed. Had some people go back and find it. It was way up under there, exactly like he said. Plus, it fit."

"Fit? You're full of it!"

"I swear. Fit our blond guy's apartment door. When we got him down to the bullpen and started questioning him, he said this to me. He said, 'Tell the kid to leave me alone now,' and perfectly described Pollock."

"Yeah?"

"Said he'd been following him around *for days*!"

J.C. Fields

J.C. Fields is a multi-award-winning and Amazon best-selling author. Many of his fourteen published novels have been awarded medals in the Reader's Favorite International Book Awards contest. His novel *A Lone Wolf* became a #1 Best Selling audiobook in March 2020.

Over the past several years, many of his numerous short stories have been featured on the YouTube Podcast Fear From the Heartland, a part of the Chilling Tales for Dark Nights network.

After a decade as an independent author, he signed a publishing contract with Vinci Books in 2024. Vinci Books is a world-class publisher created to offer independent authors the best of self-published and traditional publishing.

He is active with numerous area writing groups and serves on the board for both the Between the Pages Writers

Conference and the Ozarks Creative Writers Conference.

He lives with his wife, Connie, in Southwest Missouri.

I Am Not Crazy

They call me a murderer. I prefer to think of myself as a patron of the final journey. My clients seem satisfied. I have yet to receive a bad review. When I explained this to the jury, you would have thought the world was coming to an end. The judge banged his gavel and one of the jurists fainted. She appeared a bit too religious, maybe that's why.

During the same trial, the prosecutor referred to me as being insane. I don't do the same thing over and over expecting different results. When I repeat my actions, time after time, I know what the outcome will be. Someone will cross the river of Jordan.

Plus, I know the difference between right and wrong. I just happen to think doing the wrong thing is far more entertaining.

Now to the purpose of my missive. I was not allowed to properly relay my story to the jury, mainly due to the prosecutor begging the judge to have me restrained. Because of that, I will tell my side of the story. If the jury had heard my explanation, they would have declared me innocent, demanded my release and declared me a hero. But alas, I now find myself confined to this small room with a bed, table, chair, toilet, sink, a Big Chief tablet, and crayons. Am I insane? I'll let you decide.

Here's my story.

It all started on a dark and stormy night. I lived near a

small community where my parents grew up. My house had belonged to them and since they no longer needed it, I stayed.

The appearance of numerous headlights flashing on the curtained windows suggested I had visitors. After a profound series of knocks on the front door, I opened it. You can imagine my shock to see a sheriff's deputy pointing a gun at my face.

"Hands up, Delbert. You're under arrest."

I might have mumbled something along the lines of, "For what?"

Agitated, he screamed, "Hands up, now."

Being the intelligent individual I am, I thought it wise to do so. Next thing I know I'm in the back of a sheriff's car with my hands cuffed behind my back. I remembered a TV show where the person under arrest started talking. It didn't go well for him. So, I kept my mouth shut.

Cops and detectives were screaming at each other and rummaging through my house. I later realized they had discovered my trophies. As I sit here in this small room, my trophies have never been returned. I wonder if I can sue to have them reinstated to my care.

It was after sunrise when they placed me in a room with two detectives. I don't remember their names. They were rude and didn't take my handcuffs off.

The one on the left stared at me with his blue eyes. He said, "Want to explain why we've found ten skulls in your basement?"

"Sure, those are my trophies."

He blinked, frowned and said, "What kind of trophies?"

"They were awarded to me because I helped that individual slip the bounds of earth and start their next journey."

"So, you're telling us, they are the skulls of people you've killed?"

"No, they are the remnants of those souls who have

crossed the river of Jordan into the next realm."

The detective on the right clasped his hands together. "Did you personally help them cross the river of Jordan, Delbert?"

"Yes, of course."

"How?"

"By giving them a chance to escape these earthly constraints."

The man on the left frowned. "Did they go willingly?"

"Some did, others didn't. They complained about it not being their time. I had to disagree with them. You see, when I explained to them who I was and it was their time to cross over, they stopped arguing. There's not much you can say when I've made a decision."

The serious cop on the right leaned forward. "What gives you the power to make that decision, Delbert?"

"It's written on my driver's license."

The cop closed his eyes and shook his head. "Your license says you have the power of life and death over someone?"

"It does."

The cop on the left stood and left the room. When he returned, he held my license. "It says here your name is Delbert Thanatos."

"It is."

"How does that give you the power of life and death, Delbert?"

I smiled at him. "Thanatos is the Greek god of death."

The Alpha and Omega Affair

Author Note: The story occurs five years before The Fugitive's Trail

Alpha and Omega Consulting, LLC described their services as from the beginning to the end of employment. A large company with offices occupying floors twenty through twenty-seven of the Willis Tower in Chicago.

Their mission statement summarized the company philosophy: *We manage all personnel issues for our clients' companies from hiring to retirement, plus anything in-between.*

Unfortunately, their regional managers were being retired in a bloody and permanent fashion. Senior management contacted the FBI. And because this appeared to possibly be a serial killer, the bureau assigned Special Agent Sean Kruger. One of their more productive profilers.

Kruger shook the hand of Alpha and Omega's CEO, Burt Norman.

"Thank you for coming on such short notice, Agent Kruger. Please have a seat."

Taking in the grandeur of the man's office, Kruger said, "I understand you've had seven associates murdered over the past two years."

"Unfortunately, yes. As a rule, we don't send a team to handle a company's personnel issues. We utilize one individual, normally a regional manager, to get the job done. Cheaper for our client companies."

"And for Alpha and Omega?"

Norman frowned but did not respond right away.

"Mr. Norman, what type of companies do you deal with?"

"As a rule, ones with less than a hundred employees."

"What kind of industries?"

"Mostly manufacturers."

"All you do is contract their HR needs, correct?"

A nod from Norman.

Kruger tilted his head. "How often do you send an associate to do mass layoffs?"

"I beg your pardon."

"If a company needs to lay off most of its employees, they usually hire an outside firm to do so. How often is your company asked to provide those services?"

Norman's eyes flicked between Kruger and the large window overlooking the Chicago skyline. He remained silent for a few moments. Finally, he returned his attention to the FBI agent. "About twenty-five percent of our annual revenue is received from those functions. We don't do it for our full-service clients. We only provide those types of service to companies with their own HR department."

"Why?"

"Uh, it keeps their HR personnel from performing those types of functions. Which can result in ill will toward their HR department employees."

"How many of the murders occurred because of these types of services?"

Taking a deep breath, Norman closed his eyes. "All of them."

"And you chose not to tell the bureau this fact?"

A slow nod came from the CEO.

Kruger stood. "I'll need access to your files, Mr. Norman."

On the third day of cross-referencing the Alpha and Omega files, Kruger began to see a pattern emerge. A pattern with potential legal jeopardy for Alpha and Omega. He met with CEO Norman late on the third afternoon.

"Who assigns the associates who perform the layoffs, Mr. Norman?"

"I'm told it's a random assignment, Agent Kruger."

"Made how?"

"By computer."

"Who runs the computer?"

Norman narrowed his eyes. "What are you implying, Agent Kruger?"

"I'm not implying anything. I'm asking questions."

"No, you're implying someone inside this company is responsible for the deaths."

With a sly smile, Kruger appraised the now indignant CEO. "I didn't say that, Mr. Norman, you did. I merely asked who made the assignments."

The redness in Norman's face intensified as did the pace of his breathing. Finally, he relaxed and said, "Libby Carter. She's the head of our HR department. She is also the individual who determines who within the company has the skill set to handle these types of assignments."

"I will need to interview her."

"When?"

"Now would be a good time."

"Thank you for taking the time to meet with me, Ms.

Carter." Kruger sat at the head of a long conference table in a room next to the CEO's office.

"I didn't think I had a choice, Agent Kruger."

"Would you prefer to have an attorney present?"

"Am I a suspect?"

Tilting his head, the special agent asked, "Should you be?"

She shook her head.

"Do you want an attorney?"

"No." She paused. "I can't afford one."

This statement gave Kruger pause. He made a note and then asked, "Burt Norman indicated you are the head of the company's HR department."

"Yes."

"Do you assign the individuals who will be heading out into the field?"

She shook her head. "What gave you that idea?"

"I'm trying to determine how the company serves your clients."

"With regional managers."

"Can you explain how that works?"

"I assumed Mr. Norman would have explained."

"Indulge me, please."

"When Alpha and Omega sign a client in, let's say, Wichita, Kansas, we also hire a regional rep to handle the business. That individual is then assigned to recruit other companies to utilize our services within that geographical area."

"Is that individual responsible for all of the business within the area?"

"Yes. If they grow their client list, we authorize them to hire staff to help with the day-to-day needs."

Kruger nodded. "So, if a company contracts with this regional manager to assist with lay-offs, who does he send in?"

"The regional manager is responsible for that duty."

Staying silent, Kruger made a note. He then looked up. "What's your turnover rate?"

"In what department?"

"Regional managers."

"Negligible. Most of them receive six figure incomes."

"Okay, let me ask you another question. What happens when one retires or dies?"

"Other regional managers bid on their territories."

With a frown, Kruger asked, "What do you mean bid?"

"They will manage the clients within that geographical area for a small percentage of the revenue generated."

He sat back in his chair. "So, each regional manager is a business within itself?"

"Basically. They have to adhere to company standards, but in a sense they are independent contractors."

"Thank you, Ms. Carter."

That night in his hotel room, Kruger studied the files given to him by the CEO. One set of facts were absent, financial records. He also went over the files of the seven regional managers who had been killed. He then did a Google search. When he found the right page, a small smile came to his lips. He checked the time and made a phone call.

The Next Afternoon

Five FBI agents from the Chicago Field Office accompanied Kruger as they entered the offices of Alpha and Omega Consulting, LLC. The receptionist tried to stop them as they blew past her desk heading for the office where Kruger knew the CEO resided. The door was open, and Burt Norman could be seen at his desk with two associates sitting in front. Those men turned as the group of six FBI agents, all dressed in suits, entered the space.

Norman frowned and said, "What is the meaning of this intrusion?"

Kruger handed the man a folded document. "We are subpoenaing your financial records, Mr. Norman."

The CEO opened the page and skimmed the words. "Those are confidential records. You can't have them."

Pointing to the page, Kruger smiled. "That was signed by a federal judge this morning and it says we can." He turned to his associates. "Gentlemen, please proceed as we discussed."

As the other agents filed out of the room, Burt Norman turned to Kruger. "You could have asked for them."

"Would you have given me all the files?"

The CEO stared at Kruger for a few moments and then shook his head.

"That's the reason for the subpoena. What are we going to find, Mr. Norman?"

"I believe it's time for me to contact an attorney."

"Wise idea, sir."

Illinois Attorney General Josh Barnes looked over the files lying on his desk. "What am I looking at, Sean?"

Pointing to the flow chart Kruger had prepared from the financial records, he said, "Alpha and Omega Consulting have seven offices in the states of Ohio, Illinois, Michigan, Indiana, and Wisconsin. Ohio and Michigan have two, where the rest only have one. Those states have a large population of small manufacturers, ninety percent with fewer than one hundred employees."

"Okay, why's that important?"

"Alpha and Omega enjoys a thriving business in those areas. The commissions paid to the regional managers in those states alone amounted to over thirty million dollars."

"A substantial amount. Go on."

"If a regional manager leaves the company or dies, the region can be awarded to another regional manager who would bid with a lower commission. Substantially lower in this case."

Barnes frowned. "You're kidding."

"Nope. All seven of the regional managers who were killed earned the highest commissions of any others throughout the other states where Alpha does business. The regional managers who took those regions over are receiving a fraction of the compensation the previous managers received."

"So, who killed the original managers?"

"I think there are only two individuals who know."

"Burt Norman?"

"He's one of them."

"Who's the other."

"Libby Carter."

"Can you prove it?"

"I believe we can. As long as I can offer her a deal."

"What do you have in mind?"

Kruger told him.

"Thank you for meeting me away from your office, Ms. Carter." The two were in a Starbucks one block from the Willis Building.

"Honestly, Agent Kruger, I don't know what else I can tell you."

"Why did you ask me if you needed an attorney the last time we met?"

She stared at the FBI agent for a long time. Her lip quivered and she diverted her eyes to the coffee cup in her hand. "I was nervous."

"To be expected. But you didn't seem nervous. In fact, you were quite confident. You asked matter-of-factly, like you asked the question on a daily basis. Why is that, Ms. Carter?"

"I think I do need an attorney."

"Why, Ms. Carter?"

She stood. "I'm feeling entrapped by your insinuations."

"I haven't insinuated anything, Ms. Carter. I'm simply asking questions."

The woman stared at him, but did not move.

"Why don't you sit down, Ms. Carter, and I'll tell you a story."

She sat, but kept her purse in her lap and did not meet Kruger's gaze.

He told her what he knew. When he finished, she continued to sit there and stare out the window next to their table.

"Burt can be a charming man when he wants to be. He told me all I had to do was get the employee records for the individuals to be laid off and I could expect a nice bonus."

"How much?"

She smiled and looked at the FBI agent. "When my husband died several years ago, he left me alone with a mountain of bills. I didn't know he had a gambling problem. Mr. Norman paid them off for me."

"What did you have to do for the bonus?"

"Find out who among the employees being laid off had a criminal record."

"Did you?"

She nodded.

"And?"

"That was all, nothing else."

"Are you sure?"

She shook her head. Taking a calming breath, she said, "Once he knew who had a criminal record, he contacted them and made them a deal."

"What kind of deal?"

"If they killed the man who laid them off, they would receive an airline ticket to any country they wanted. Plus, they would receive fifty thousand dollars."

"Seven men took him up on the offer?"

She nodded again.

"Ms. Carter, you could be considered an accomplice to murder."

"I know."

"Will you be willing to testify against Burt Norman?"

She looked at him with narrowed eyes. "Only if I can get a deal."

"It's your lucky day."

The arrest of Burt Norman occurred two days later. Agents from the Chicago Field Office did the honors while Kruger watched. The Special Agent in Charge of Chicago, Bob Simmons, stood next to him.

"How solid is our case against Norman?"

"Granite."

A small frown appeared on the man's face. "Based on the Carter woman's testimony?"

"Nope."

Simmons chuckled. "Knowing you, Sean, you have something else up your sleeve."

"The written statement from each of the men he hired to kill the regional managers."

The Scream

The planning for this project began a little over three years ago. My seed money from investors amounted to $200,000. When I promised a 250% return on their money, the greedy bastards jumped all over it. Big talk, right?

Not in the slightest. I have access to over one hundred and twenty million dollars in famous paintings. From Old Masters to Abstract Expressionism, I have this planned down to the exact paintings I am taking and who is going to buy them.

As you might already have surmised, I'm an art thief. One of the best. Ever.

Currently, I am hiding in my sanctuary deep in the basement of this museum. It took me a year to prepare this room. Now all I have to do is wait for the exhibition hall to close and I will emerge. It's Saturday night. The place is closed tomorrow and Monday. The so-called security guard greedily accepted my offer and is now winging his way, first class, I might add, to an island in the Mediterranean. Which means, the building is empty. Except for myself.

At midnight, a small transit van will arrive and park at the loading dock. The driver will exit the vehicle, lock it, walk away, and disappear. He will never see me. He, too, has been well paid.

Not one of the individuals helping me knows who I am. Nor do they know the other participants of my plan. It was designed that way. Everyone got their instructions via text message or USPS. If any of them gets caught, they can't identify who hired them. Only I know the entirety of the full scheme.

The hour of midnight has struck. I am leaving the sanctuary of my bunker deep within the lower basement of the museum. It is now time to move the art pieces to the loading dock.

I chose this particular museum because it contains three versions of Edvard Munch's *The Scream*. My client wants all three. Combined, their value at auction would be close to 500 million US dollars. However, they will never see the auction block.

He offered me 120 million to obtain them for his private collection. The world will never see them again, until he dies. This arrangement is an excellent deal for me. I will give my investors their fifty million and I will walk away with a cool seventy million, tax free dollars. At which time, I, too, will disappear.

If you are unfamiliar with *The Scream*, it is the painting with the man standing in a road with his hands pressed to his face. The distorted figure along with the blood red sky in the background, gives the portrait an eerie persona.

It is said Edvard Munch possessed a haunted soul with a family history of mental illness. Looking at his paintings, I would have to agree with the assessment.

The paintings are also quite fragile. They are stored in a refrigerated storage vault on the same level as my sanctuary. I haven't looked at them yet, but I know they are there. I have access to the facility's computer inventory.

The lock on the storage vault is electronic and easy to circumvent. I gained admittance to the room in less than ten minutes.

Darkness within the space is complete. A motion detecting device actuates the lighting and the paintings are revealed. My senses are assaulted by the images. A shiver runs up my spine as I gaze at the portraits. A feeling of vertigo attacks my senses, and I almost lose my balance. I lean back against the door frame, preventing my collapse to the floor. I close my eyes, but the spinning remains. Finally, I am able to stabilize myself and gaze upon the paintings.

This close to them, I feel the author's madness. It is like an invisible force pushing down on my psyche. The exhaustion is oppressive. I am forced to back out of the room. The feeling instantly dissipates. My research on the paintings did not indicate the presence of a supernatural aura. Is it my imagination, or something else?

How long I stood outside the room is something I will never know. Time stood still for me. Finally, I reentered. My world swirled with all the same colors of Munch's nightmare.

Closing my eyes, the vertigo returns. Only this time I am standing on the road with the swirling colors in the sky. I can see two men standing on the boulevard ahead, and I call out to them. They neither turn or acknowledge my presence.

Maybe that was what Munch was trying to relay in his painting. We are all utterly alone, with no one to hear our screams.

Eventually, I opened my eyes. The familiar scene of the storage room returns. The paintings remain where I left them. It is time to move the paintings. I pick one up to move it to the hall.

Darkness descends and the vertigo returns. I am spinning. I have no sense of up or down, only a circling sensation. Like swirling into a drain. Then, total blackness.

I'm not sure how long I remained unconscious. When I finally opened my eyes, I had to question my own sanity. I am pressing my hands against my face trying to scream. My face is thin as I stare at the vault door.

I realize…I am inside the painting.

R.H. BURKETT

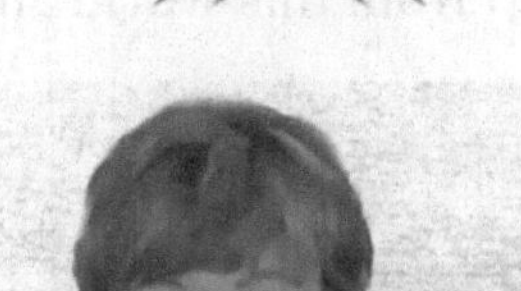

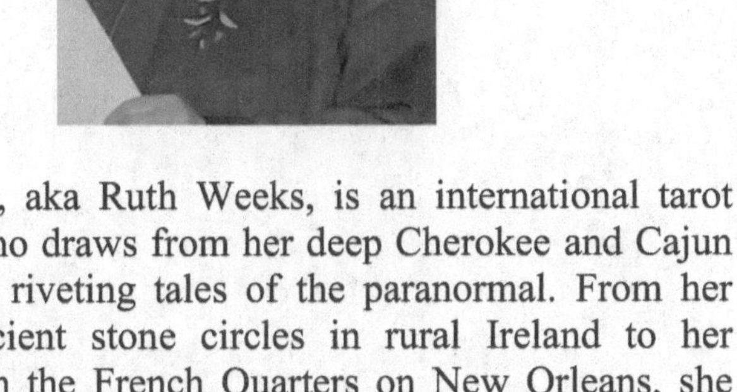

R. H. Burkett, aka Ruth Weeks, is an international tarot card reader who draws from her deep Cherokee and Cajun roots to write riveting tales of the paranormal. From her travels to ancient stone circles in rural Ireland to her explorations in the French Quarters on New Orleans, she tells stories that encompass her love of all things mystical.

Her latest release *Broom Flyer's Tales and Spells* is a compilation of her short stories, one of which was nominated for a 2023 Spur Award (Western Writers of America). Her first novel, *Soldiers In the Mist* was voted Ozark Writers League (OWL) 2012 Best Book of the year. Her second novel, *Daughter of the Howling Moon,* was the Oklahoma Writers Federation (OWFI) 2015 Book of the Year.

As a child, Ruth was fascinated by stories about her Grandmother Ely, who was part Cherokee and part Cajun.

That was the inspiration for her adopting the handle Witchy Woman. She currently lives in Springdale, Arkansas, with her familiar, Fred. Check out her website rhburkett.com and follow her author page, where you can watch videos of the author talking about her travels, her heritage, and the people she meets both from this world and the next.

Sooie Pig

"She did it."

"Bet my badge on it."

"Think we'll ever prove it?"

Detective Johnson shrugged. "What makes you think I want to? The guy was evil."

"Not relevant. It's our duty to catch the bad guys."

"Dani Mason is no bad guy."

"True, never-the-less, she did it."

Well, of course I did it. Someone had to.

At times the wheels of justice move painfully slow. I just sped things up a little, that's all.

Did I feel remorseful? Only if caught. A rat-bastard beat the soup out of my best friend, killed her dog, and threatened her little boy. The creep deserved to die.

"Earth to Dani."

I shook loose from my thoughts. "Oh, sorry, Jeannie."

"Trying to figure out who killed Tommy Whitmire? Good luck with that. You know the police suspect a woman, don't you?"

"Spit it out, Jean. What you really mean is I'm their number one suspect."

"Sorry. I was trying to be considerate."

"Not your forte, girlfriend."

"Did you? Kill him, I mean."

Now why would I admit to murder, especially to a nitwit like Jeannie?

"Yes, Jeannie. I poisoned the guy, stabbed him ten times, shot him through the head, then buried him in a shallow grave so farmer Brown's dog could dig him up."

She laughed. "Okay. I surrender. Besides, no one truly knows what happened. They can't find the body."

"Now, see? That's exactly why I don't understand any of this hoopla. Why do the cops even think a crime was committed? Maybe the rat scurried off to buy cheese or take a vacation in some garbage dump somewhere."

"The massive pool of blood found in his driveway might have something to do with it."

"Oh yeah, there is that."

Darn it all. I knew I should've taken time to Clorox the cement. The only flaw in my plan. Well, not exactly. There was one detail that could prove problematic—the body stuffed in my freezer.

"You're off the planet again, my friend. What is wrong with you?"

"It's not every day I have cops hauling me in for questioning, Jeannie. Excuse me if I'm a little scatterbrained."

"Dani, sometimes your sarcasm hurts. Everyone in this town knows you and Tommy had a checkered past."

"Checkered? He beat the stuffing out of my best friend. He would've done the same to her son if her dalmatian didn't take a hunk out of his leg, which, by the way, he shot dead. I hated him."

"And that is why you're the main suspect."

"The jerk was a drunk. He sold crack to teenagers. Had a police record a block long. But I'm the one getting blamed for some phantom crime? Give me a break."

"No, give *me* a break. You made no bones about how much you detested him. Shouted at the top of your lungs how if he ever touched Patty again he'd be sorry."

"Never said I'd kill him."

"Oh, whatever. I'm out of here."

Jeannie thought she was my best friend. Not even close. My best bud was Patty Holiday.

Patty and I became best friends in the sixth grade when I told her how cool her last name was. From that day forward, we were joined at the hip. Patty was smart as a whip. Accelerated classes all through school. But for all her smarts, Patty had an Achilles's heel—men. More accurately, bad men.

As often happens, we lost track of one another when Patty went away to college. Fate, however, reunited us when she moved back years later with a baby. Deadbeat Dad split never to be seen again. Lost and downtrodden, she knocked on my door one night and never left. We vowed to always have each other's back.

Neither Patty nor I ever dreamed how sadistic and mean her new boyfriend was until it was too late. Tommy used Patty like a punching bag more than once. It wasn't until he went after her little boy, that the shit hit the fan.

Damn straight I killed Tommy Whitmire. If the shoe were on the other foot, Patty would do the same for me.

I stopped and picked up her pain pills before heading home. We had a job to do.

"Your mom come and pick up John Junior?"

"She just left."

"What she say about your black eye and broken arm?"

"Kill the bastard."

Gotta love Mama Holiday.

"What did the cops say? They think you did it, don't they?"

"They asked a bunch of questions. I had answers for each one. They're fishing. No body, no crime. Right?"

"Right. Speaking of bodies. What are we going to do with Popsicle Tommy?"

"I was rather hoping you had a solution."

"Well… actually, I do have an idea. But it's far-fetched."

"Will it work?"

"One hundred percent."

"Then I don't care how crazy it is. Shoot."

"Bourbon first."

"You shouldn't drink with those pills."

"Oh, it's not just for me."

This was going to be good.

"Hogs?"

"Yes. Virgil Ray told me a sure-fire way to get rid of a body is throw it in a hog pen. They'll eat everything except the teeth."

"Virgil Ray, the old biker dude?"

"Yes. He was an MP in the army. He knows what he's talking about. Said hogs like the fermented smell of bourbon, especially if it's mixed in sugar." She held up a jar full of the stuff. "I just made us some hog hooch to draw those piggies in."

"Good enough for me. Where's the nearest hog farm?"

"Over the state line about an hour from here."

"It'll be dark soon. Let's get Tommy loaded and ready to go."

"Oh… My… God, Dani! You didn't tell me you folded him in half!"

"He wouldn't fit in the freezer otherwise."

"He's a solid block of ice, weighs a ton. No way we can lift him out."

I searched my toolbox. Finally found a hammer and chisel. "This will work."

"Oh, Jesus! You're not?"

"Got any better ideas? Bring that washtub over here."

I chiseled away at Tommy. Patty threw each piece into the tub. A foot here. A hand there. Each solid thud made both of us cringe. A few more shots of bourbon, and we were good to go. Patty helped me lift the tub into the trunk and slipped behind the wheel.

"You've been drinking, better let me drive."

We both broke into hysterics. A DWI was the least of our worries.

The hog farm wasn't hard to find. We just followed our noses.

"Holy crap! Stinks worse than any chicken farm on earth."

Patty stood lookout.

I threw each thawed-out piece of Tommy into the hog pen and watched the frenzy begin.

"Sooie pig!"

Patty broke the silence on the way back home.

"Dani? You know we'll go to hell for this."

"God forgives."

"You're a diabolical villain."

"Look me in the eye and tell me Tommy wouldn't have killed your innocent child."

"I can't."

"Exactly. You think God wanted that?"

"No."

"We never speak of this again *ever*. Deal?

"Deal."

"Should we pull them over and arrest her now?"

Detective Johnson shook his head. "Nope."

"But boss, she just…

"Tommy Whitmire was the devil incarnate. Besides, no body, no crime. Case closed."

"But she did it."

Johnson smiled.

"Did what?"

Susan Keene

Susan was born in California but moved to Alton, Illinois as a child and considers it her hometown. After high school she received training and was licensed as a Radiological Technician. Although her love has always been literature and writing, she has had many jobs she thinks gave her a well-rounded view of the world. She uses that knowledge in her fiction writing.

She has two popular cozy mystery series, The Kate Nash Mysteries and the Arizona Summers Mysteries. She likes to make each novel in her series such that it will stand alone, but says they are more fun to read in order.

Her newest novel, *Buried in Time* is the fifteenth she's written. Susan is branching out in subject matter. This is the first book in her Alexa Ford Cozy Mystery series, and she adds the twist of paranormal.

Susan writes full time, but loves to spend time with

friends, her daughter and grandchildren and her two mini-dachshunds and a Min Pin.

She loves to hear from her readers. You can reach her at: susan@susankeeneauthor.com

While you are there, please sign up for her newsletter which will start in September,

BENEATH THE SNOWY GROUND

Elaine Durham had a reputation in Barton Row. Some people made fun of her and called her the *treasure hunter*. Others wondered why a young beautiful girl would want to spend all of her time alone. The rest of the teens her age met at the mall, saw the latest movies, and had slumber parties. Elaine seemed not to notice.

"It's a hobby," she'd tell anyone who asked. She'd been a loner since her father died in an auto accident. Her mom, try as she might, wanted to keep the family together, but it wasn't working.

Danny, her brother, had gone across the state to college. It left her alone with her mom, who no longer took an active role in her own life, much less Elaine's. Elaine used to go with her dad every Saturday to search for old coins, civil war buttons, and any other treasure they could dig up.

On this particular Saturday morning, she decided to cross the eastern edge of the old Blackstone farm. It was late November and the first snow crunched under her feet as she walked. The old house, which sat in the middle of the farm, had been abandoned for decades. She'd had it on her list of places she wanted to search for a long time. She had to wait until the first freeze due to the snake population in places like the crumbling foundation of the old house.

Her detector had never picked up much on the part of the farm closest to her house, a few corroded coins, a horseshoe, the occasional piece of farm equipment.

Nothing worth keeping. But today, something felt different. The air hung still and heavy despite the snow she could feel soaking through her boots and all three of her pairs of socks.

About fifty yards from the old foundation, she turned on her detector and began to scan. After a good ten minutes, as she began to second guess her decision, the detector's monotonous hum suddenly pitched higher. Elaine stopped, sweeping back over the spot. The signal strengthened.

She knelt and took out her small garden trowel, carefully removing the top layer of snow before she could begin to dig in the ground, which was more frozen than she thought it would be. Twenty minutes and six inches down, her trowel clinked against something solid. Her heart quickened; she brushed the dirt away with a new excitement.

A glint of gold and a flash of red caught the morning light.

It was a ring—delicate yet ornate, the gold band was tarnished with age. The weight and ornate design told her it was old and expensive. At its center sat a ruby as big as her thumb nail. It was surrounded by diamonds; they were half the size of the ruby, but when the sun caught them, they twinkled. It was a miracle considering how much dirt clung to it.

"My goodness," Elaine whispered. This wasn't the usual discarded junk. This was valuable—historically significant, perhaps.

She slipped it onto her palm for a closer look. The moment the metal touched her skin, the world tilted.

A flash of white—a girl's dress among trees. Running footsteps. Heavy breathing. Fear.

Elaine gasped and nearly dropped the ring. The vision had come and gone in an instant, but it left her shaking.

"Hello? Are you all right?"

Elaine turned to see a boy, a little older than her,

watching her from several yards away. He looked like he was in his late teens or early twenties. He had a deep tan, not a sunbathing suntan, but one someone got from spending lots of time outside, maybe a lifeguard. He leaned on a walking stick. It didn't look like he needed it to walk.

"I'm fine," she called, instinctively closing her fingers around the ring. "I lost my balance."

He approached slowly. "You're Elaine Durham, right, the girl who hunts for treasure."

She nodded, standing. "It's a hobby."

"You can't dig on this land, it's private. "His voice was neither threatening nor friendly. "This ground isn't meant to be disturbed."

"It's public property now," Elaine said. "Has been since the county took it over in the nineties."

The boy—she still didn't know his name—looked toward the ruins of the foundation. "You found something, didn't you? I can see it in your face."

Elaine looked toward home and hesitated. The ring felt unnaturally warm in her closed fist.

"I should introduce myself," he said. "Mike Blackstone. My grandfather owned this estate."

The name struck Elaine like a physical blow. Everyone in town knew the Blackstone story—the wealthy family whose fortune collapsed after the stock market crash of 1929, followed by the mysterious disappearance of their young daughter.

"Charlotte," Elaine said, not meaning to blurt it out. "Charlotte Blackstone. She went missing in 1929."

Mike gave her a dirty look. "So, you know the story."

"Only what everyone knows. That she vanished. That they never found her."

"They never found her because they weren't meant to." Mike looked at Elaine's closed fist. "What did you find?"

Before she could answer, she felt it again—the ring pulsing with warmth, and then—

The same white dress, now torn and muddied. Moonlight filtering through autumn leaves. A girl's hand clutching something that gleamed red. The sound of shouting in the distance.

"Elaine?" Blackstone's voice seemed to come from far away.

Elaine opened her eyes. She was on her knees, though she didn't remember falling. "I found a ring," she said, her voice hoarse. "And I think... I think it's showing me something."

For a long moment, Mike said nothing. Then, as if an afterthought, he said, "My family never spoke of what happened that night. Not even my grandfather. Only that Charlotte was gone, along with my great-grandmother's ruby ring."

Elaine slowly opened her hand, revealing the ring on her palm. The ruby seemed darker now, almost black in the center.

The young man stared at it, his face draining of color. "After all these years..."

"What happened to her, Mike?"

He shook his head. "I don't know. But local legends say the ring was cursed. That it showed visions to those who wore it. Charlotte saw something she shouldn't have."

Elaine looked down at the ring. "I'm seeing her. Running and afraid."

"Don't," Mike said sharply. "Don't put it on."

But the ring had already slipped onto Elaine's finger—she wasn't sure if she'd done it herself or if the ring had somehow moved of its own accord.

This time, the vision consumed her completely.

Charlotte, running through these same woods, the ring clutched in her small fist. The crash of branches behind her. Men's voices calling her name. Her breath coming in terrified gasps. The ground ahead opening into a sudden drop—the old quarry that hadn't been used in years.

Charlotte stopping at the edge, turning to face her pursuers, the faces of men she recognized. Family men. Trusted men.

"Give it back, Charlotte," one said, extending his hand. "That ring doesn't belong to you."

"It showed me what you did," the girl whispered, her voice breaking. "It showed me everything."

The men exchanged glances. "No one will believe you," another said softly. "Just give it back, and we can forget this happened."

Charlotte looked down at the ring, then at the dark waters of the quarry below. She made her choice—

The vision cut off abruptly. Elaine found herself staring into Mike Blackstone's face. He had gripped her wrist, pulling the ring from her finger.

"Enough," he said. "Some things should stay buried."

Elaine's heart hammered in her chest. "Charlotte knew something. Something about those men—your family and others. The ring showed her. What did she see?" Elaine asked.

Mike released her wrist. "I don't know. But the night she disappeared there was a meeting at our house. Important men from town. When it ended, Charlotte was gone. They said she ran away."

Elaine looked down at the ring now lying between them on fallen leaves. "But she didn't, did she? She didn't run away."

The wind picked up, sending dead leaves swirling around them. In the distance, the ruins of the Blackstone house stood silently.

"Take it," Mike said suddenly. "Take the ring. Maybe it's time someone knew the truth."

As Elaine's fingers closed around the ring once more, she felt the weight of a long-buried secret—and the responsibility that came with it. Whatever had happened to Charlotte Blackstone in 1929, the ruby ring was ready to reveal at last.

Here's what we know… whatever happened to Charlotte, the ring remained at the top of the hill near the farmhouse where she lived with her family.

The ring told Charlotte horrible deeds a group of townsmen were guilty of.

What would you do?

At this point, it seems as though she has only two choices--one, to jump to certain death in the quarry, or two, to stand her ground. Turn to face the group of men, some of who she knew, and face her destiny.

But remember, she has, in her possession, a magic ring. Could she use it to escape her fate?

"Do you believe if the ring revealed all of the evil these men did that it would somehow save Charlotte?"

"I don't know what to think," Mike said. "Maybe we could study it together and finally solve the mystery."

Elaine smiled. "Maybe we can."

Can A Box Be Magic

Mrs. Allen opened the door and greeted Officer Hadit. "Well, Mrs. Allen, what now, another cat keeping you up at night?"

She didn't answer. She walked into the living room. "This is my problem," she said.

He followed her eyes to the mantel where a blue gift box sat. "Are you talking about the box?"

"Yes, when I went out to get the morning paper, it was on the porch." She pointed to it.

Officer Hadit reached to pick up the box.

Mrs. Allen slapped his hand away, much harder than she needed to. "Look, it says DO NOT OPEN."

"You called me here to look at a box you won't open because it says not to, but you don't know who sent it or what is in it?"

"Well, Officer, that isn't all of it. I've had it several days. The first day, I sat it on the dining room table. Every time I leave the room it's in, it moves. It has moved from the mantel to the kitchen table to the dining room table. Once I went into the bathroom and it had moved to my vanity."

He turned back to the box, it was gone. It was on the dining room table. "How did you do that?"

She shook her head. "You turn your back on it, and it moves. It has been all over this house, upstairs, downstairs, and even on the back porch."

He walked over and picked up the box. "I bet it's a prank. What is happening here is not possible." He picked up the box and shook it. "It's empty," he said.

He sat the box back on the table and peeled the DO NOT DISTURB sign off. Nothing happened. No sound came from the box, nothing was inside. The only thing different was Officer Hadit was gone.

Mrs. Allen nearly fainted.

There sat the box, open and empty. She walked into the kitchen to get a drink of water and there sat the box, on the kitchen counter.

The lid was back on, and the note the officer pulled off was back on the box. It now said, "THANK YOU, ONE MORE."

The old lady collapsed on the couch. Several days went by and the box didn't move. It remained on the counter. A few times she went outside and sat, giving the box time to move, but it didn't.

She called the police department to inquire about Officer Hadit. They told her no officer had been dispatched to her home. And there wasn't now, nor was there ever, an officer named Hadit.

The box began to move again. She put it out with the trash and watched as the truck took it away.

It came back.

She threw it in the river downtown.

It came back.

It always had a note attached. The note had changed. It now read, "ONE MORE, YOU KNOW WHO."

For two days, she thought and thought about what the note could mean. Was it saying she could pick someone she wished was not around and he would be gone, like Officer Hadit?

A sound began to come out of the box. She couldn't describe it as music. It was a mixture of melody and sort of a siren sound. She knew what it meant. She needed to name someone.

She named her ex-husband. Martin. She'd only been married to him for five years, and it was in the sixties, but he never left her alone. He stalked her, ran off every boyfriend she'd ever had, and told lies about her so he could have custody of their son when they broke up.

Then there were the bruises. He would try to hit her in places that didn't show, but she thought everyone knew. She lost every court battle because he was a trial lawyer, and she was a housewife.

She couldn't remember if she said Martin's name aloud. It had been over fifty-years, yet anytime she thought of him, it was with anger and loss. Anger at what he did to her and the loss of her son, Martin, who had turned against her years before.

She woke up in the middle of the night. The beautiful blue box sat next to her. A new note attached read, "HE IS GONE. YOU ARE FREE. THERE IS NO REASON TO SPEND ANOTHER UNHAPPY DAY."

She turned over and when she turned back, the box was gone.

Fun With Dick and Jane

On a dark and stormy night, twelve-year-olds, Dick and Jane Jones were wet, scared, tired, and chilled. They moved into a night as dark as India ink. Weeds tore at their legs, wind blew so hard it pushed water into their eyes with such force, even the lightning seemed as dim as a flashlight with a battery soon to die.

They had no idea if the killers had followed them.

They knew their Aunt Joyce lived on the other side of the woods. They had run out of their home until the woods behind their house hid them. The kids were accompanied by the screams of their mother and the sounds of the gun shots as they ripped through their father's body.

Dick pulled his twin sister under a tree. The rain had stopped, the wind died down, and Dick believed it safe enough for them to stop and catch their breath.

Jane buried her head in her brother's shoulder and whispered, "What do you think happened back there? Are Mom and Dad both dead?"

"Of course they're dead, but why? Who would want to kill them?" Dick didn't expect an answer to his questions.

Dick, always the adult, remained quiet for several minutes before he said, "I'd say it was a robbery. I saw the bald-headed man take Dad's watch. The tall guy had a bag. I saw the other guy take Mom's ring."

Jane stood back and looked at Dick. "Do you think they knew we were in the house?"

"Hard to say," he answered. "I hope not. I think it depends on how long they stayed and what they saw before they left. The cake dishes were in the sink, and our iPads were on my bed."

Jane began to cry. It was difficult for Dick to understand her words through the sobs. "Do you have any idea where we are?"

Lightning split the sky horizontally. It was the most light they'd had since they left their home. "I'm almost sure Aunt Joyce's house is over there." He pointed to the north.

The rain seemed to be over. The sky lightened up and the kids found the path to their aunt's house. As far back as they could remember, they had run through the woods to visit their aunt.

They ran to her front porch and were about to ring the doorbell when Dick grabbed Jane's hand and pulled her back. "Look, it's the men from our house. They are talking loud. I think I can catch most of it," Dick said.

One of the men said, "Just pay us and we'll get out of here."

Their aunt asked, "Where are those incorrigible children?"

The short man pointed outside. "We heard them take out the back door. Hopefully they were struck by lightning."

"Gentleman, don't speak ill of the heirs to twenty million dollars. Especially to their new guardian."

Dick and Jane looked at one another. They linked hands and ran back toward the woods. Once they were clear of the house Jane said, "Did you hear that? She had Mom and Dad killed. For MONEY!"

"It is she who should be dead." Dick yelled angrily.

With their heads hung in despair and their hearts breaking in two, they trudged back toward the house where their mother and father lay in pools of blood in the living room.

Jane called 911, and within minutes sirens wailed in the

distance. The closer the sounds came, the more upset the kids became.

Hours later they'd told police what they knew about the crime, and how they went to their aunt's and found the murderers there.

When asked if they heard or saw anything while they looked in the window at Joyce's house, they both looked down at their feet. With proper inflections they each said they heard nothing as they hid outside under Aunt Joyce's window. They cried and told the police their aunt was the closest relative they had. "The reason we came back here was to see if we could do anything for our parents," Dick said.

They were escorted to the back of a squad car after extensive questions about what they saw and heard while the killers were in their home.

A detective, Nathan Mars, told them someone would call their aunt and have her come get them at the police station.

After what seemed like hours, the man returned with a sad demeaner and tone. "Sorry to lay anymore on you kids, but your aunt is dead. We don't know what happened, but we will find out.

"Meanwhile, we have called the Division of Family Services. They'll take you somewhere safe. Do you know any other family members?" He turned away and slowly turned back. "I'm sorry about your parents and about your aunt."

When asked if they knew any other family members, neither child answered.

They sat quietly and studied their feet.

Once the cop was well out of sight and sound, they looked at one another and smiled.

CLARISSA WILLIS

Clarissa (Chrissy) Willis, a lively spirit with a creative flair, is the daughter of a minister and a drama teacher. Her rich imagination has fueled her passion for speaking and writing. Having called nine states home, she boasts a successful career as a senior vice president of publishing at a major corporation and has dedicated over 40 years to education. Growing up in Little Rock, Arkansas, her childhood was filled with adventurous stories and misadventures, from the humorous attempt on her brother's life—which she insists was not her fault—to mischievous antics like robbing the church collection plate. Her vibrant personality and colorful past make her a truly fun and inspiring figure.

Meet the creative force behind Solander Press—a lively company that helps authors bring their stories to life for kids and grown-ups alike. She's an award-winning author, having snagged the Will Rogers Medallion for her captivating book *Fast as the Wind: The Story of Johnny Fry, Pony Express Rider.* She is also the author of *The Three Little Pigs and the Not So Big Bad Wolf* and *Bloomers on Pike's Peak: The Story of Julia Archibald Holmes*. Fun fact: *Bloomers on Pike's Peak* earned a 2024 Will Rogers Medallion and was the only finalist for the 2024 Willa Literary Award!

When she's not busy writing or celebrating her books, she's sneaking off to pen spooky tales—her own mental health secret sauce. She's also active in the writing community, serving on the boards of the Between the Pages Writers' Conference and the Ozark Creative Writers Conference. Living in the scenic mountains of northwest Arkansas with her two adorable dogs, George and Gracie, she's always crafting fresh stories and enjoying an occasional trip to faraway places.

Conspiracy Theories

"What do you mean, work? We've planned this trip for two years," Cassie exclaimed. "This is the event of a lifetime, a total solar eclipse. The next one is in 20 years, and we would have to go 1000 miles north to see it. We will be dead the next time it happens in the south."

"Cassie, it's double overtime. I can't pass that up for anything. You can go with Spencer. I know you've had a crush on him since the sixth grade."

"I won't go with him, Steph. Your brother is crazy."

"Aw, he's not that bad. Gotta go. Tell me all about it when you get back." The cell phone in her hand went dead as the call disconnected.

Her best friend, Stephanie, backed out of the trip two days before the total solar eclipse in Arkansas. Now, with her car in the shop, Cassie had to endure four hours in a beat-up truck with her best friend's brother, Spencer, and his wild ideas.

It won't be that bad, she told herself as she hopped in the truck. From the minute he picked her up until they finally made it from Oklahoma to Arkansas, all he did was talk about conspiracy theories.

At one point, Cassie asked, "If you are convinced there is a plot for technology to take over the world, why don't you move to Alaska and live off the grid?"

"Ha, ha. Don't think for a minute, Cassie, that I haven't

thought about it. There is no one to stop the rampant proliferation of technology," he said.

"Speaking of stopping, how about a potty break? I want to grab some bottled water, too," Cassie pleaded.

"Sure, but stay away from commercial water. The government puts things in it to make you sterile."

"Of course they do." Cassie rolled her eyes as he pulled into a small convenience store.

"You headed to the total eclipse?" A lady asked her as she walked toward the bathroom.

"Yep," Cassie called over her shoulder.

Cassie bought two bottles of water and some sour candy. She remembered it was Spencer's favorite candy when they were kids, so once back in the truck, she handed it to him.

He devoured it all in one bite. "I can't believe you remembered how much I love this stuff." Spencer's green eyes met hers.

"Ha," Cassie replied. "I've got your number, Spencer. You won't drink bottled water, but you will eat sour bites filled with preservatives!"

"You caught me." He grinned and started the truck.

Spencer was right about one thing. Going to a remote spot was a great idea. The crowds in the parking lot at the elementary school in Cedarville were sparse. He had picked the perfect location to watch the total eclipse. About 75 people sat in chairs and on the hoods of their cars. She had heard a news report that thousands of people were expected in Arkansas to watch the event. He pulled into a parking space.

"Remember," Spencer whispered, "if you see anything unusual, head for the truck."

Cassie grabbed a folding chair from the truck bed and selected a spot. She took her glasses out and waited. In the distance, someone strummed a guitar, and a few folks sang along. Children laughed and played in the grass. A woman sold freshly baked cookies. All around her, families ate picnic lunches. Dogs sat by their owners, hoping for a snack or a bite of a sandwich.

She had waited years for this day. It was awesome except, of course, having to ride with Spencer. He was adorable, but she wished he weren't crazy. He finally joined her, carrying a chair and sporting a pair of homemade eclipse glasses. They were held together with masking tape.

"You made your own glasses?" She tried not to roll her eyes.

"Yes, the ones they sold in the stores could be defective. What if this is a plot to blind all the people watching? Your eclipse glasses may not protect you at all. They tried depopulation with Covid, and now imagine millions of people all over the Northern Hemisphere suddenly blind."

"Yeah, we saw that movie. I still have nightmares because of you. You forced your sister to watch *Night of the Triffids* when you got stuck babysitting us. The entire world was blinded by alien trees." Cassie shuddered when she remembered how mad they got at him for making them sit all the way through the old horror movie at the drive-in while he made out with some girl.

"But what if..." Spencer looked down at her.

"Enough," she roared. He winked and put his chair down close to hers.

"Ten minutes to go," he whispered.

She quickly lost all hope that he would sit quietly. First, he made a comment about a nearby family from Mars. He had just begun explaining how the government faked the moon landing when a hush fell over the crowd.

It finally happened. The eclipse started slowly. First, only a small portion of the sun was covered. She watched in awe as the total eclipse, a moment of beauty and suspense, played out before her.

The darkness grew around her, and time stood still. The utter quiet amazed Cassie. No birds sang, no insect noise.

There was complete silence followed by total darkness. She couldn't help but reach for Spencer's hand and squeeze it. He squeezed back. She let go of his hand and took a deep breath.

Slowly, the light returned, and in a few minutes, it was sunny again. She took off her glasses and stood up. Where was Spencer? He sat inside the truck. When did that happen? She looked around, and everyone was leaving. It was still deathly quiet. No one talked or laughed. No lady sold baked goods. No children played in the nearby grass. People silently walked to their cars and drove away. Left behind were chairs, coolers, and even a few pets looking for their owners. *This is weird.* Her confusion escalated.

She put her chair in the truck bed and joined Spencer inside the cab. "That was awesome," Cassie exclaimed.

"That was awesome," he replied without inflection.

"See, nothing happened. Let's go home."

"Let's go home," Spencer answered in a monotone. During the first twenty minutes of the ride, Cassie enjoyed the silence. Spencer didn't say one word. There was no talk about aliens, government conspiracies, or anything.

"Are you mad at me for criticizing your theories?"

Spencer didn't answer. When they got to the turnoff for the main highway, Spencer kept going straight down the road in the opposite direction.

"Hey, you missed the turnoff." He didn't answer her. "Enough, Spencer, you're scaring me."

"You are scaring me," he said flatly.

Bored, Cassie turned on the radio, and the emergency broadcast network looped a message. A monotone voice repeated over and over.

"*Operation Artificial Intelligence was 98% successful. The remaining 2% of the unaffected population will be taken to processing plants for A.I. implementation.*"

"Spencer, did you hear that? If this is your idea of a joke, I am not laughing."

"This unit is now referred to as S-54a." Spencer looked at her with hollow eyes.

Cassie tried to open the car door and jump out, but the handle on the door had been removed.

He drove up to a large gate surrounding what looked like a large factory. On the fence was a sign that read: Artificial Intelligence Processing Center.

Cassie screamed.

The Casket Bride

Looking over the ship's bow, Michelle Delacroix sighed. After the long voyage, she had arrived in the French colony of New Orleans. She was one of twenty-four mail-order brides sent from France to marry men they had never met. Each woman could bring a small trunk or casket that held all her worldly goods.

Michelle, filled with serene anticipation and a sense of liberation from the confines of Paris, eagerly looked forward to her new life. Unlike her fellow travelers, who were conscripted for the journey, she had volunteered willingly, her heart yearning for her intended to find her soon.

As guests at a local boarding house, the women had no choice but to sit in the parlor and wait for their new husbands to claim them.

"This heat is awful," Cherie commented.

"It is so primitive here," Renee chimed in.

Michelle didn't respond. He was near, and she could feel him. She looked up and locked eyes with a tall, dark-haired man walking toward her.

"I am Simon Montage, and I seek a Miss Delacroix."

Mesmerized, she stood up. He gently took her hand and kissed the back of it.

"Welcome, mon chéri," he whispered.

The trip to his home lasted about an hour, and as they traveled, Simon enjoyed sharing details about his property.

The carriage turned onto a long, well-maintained driveway and revealed a stunning house hidden among the trees, a peaceful sight that captivated Michelle.

"Your new home."

"It is lovely, and I expect to spend hours exploring the property."

"I have only one request. You must never go out at night. It is not safe; many dangerous predators roam the night."

She smiled and nodded.

They entered the house, and he introduced the housekeeper: "Arceneaux, this is my new bride, Michelle Delacroix."

The creole woman glared at Michelle and mumbled, "Loup-garou."

"That is enough. She is your new mistress," Simon reprimanded.

Arceneaux looked at Simon and said, "We have prepared a feast for your arrival. Father Durant is waiting in the parlor."

"We are to be married now?" she asked.

"Yes, your room is at the top of the stairs. Freshen up," he replied. "Tonight, you will be my bride."

She did as he requested and walked into the parlor an hour later, wearing a lace collar over her pink silk gown. After the ceremony and the magnificent feast prepared by Simon's staff, Michelle feigned exhaustion and went to bed.

She hoped Simon did not expect her to fulfill her wifely duties the first night they were wed. However, when he came to her bed a few hours later, she obliged, relieved that he departed to his own bedchamber once he was finished.

When she awoke the following morning, Simon was gone. To her relief, Arceneaux was nowhere in sight. Michelle made tea and quickly laced it with the powder she had brought from France. She hoped the alchemist Marie-

Anne de La Ville had created what she needed. Tonight, there was a full moon; it was almost time. She would know once and for all if the powder worked.

Simon returned to the house at noon, and her eyes met his. "I trust you slept well, my dear. Arceneaux has left us, but you can hire a new housekeeper soon. And perhaps a nanny as well. I am keen to start a family as soon as possible."

"Whatever you wish," she replied sweetly.

An hour before sunrise, she woke up to find Simon had returned to his room again. Wearing her black cloak, she quietly slipped out of the house into the woods. The black panther inside her surfaced. Into the night, she ran, finally free.

Michelle no longer wished to live in their world. The powder had done its magic, and the spell was cast. She could now remain her true self. Three months later, she gave birth to two male cubs, and she watched as they grew and thrived where they belonged in the wild with their own kind.

Simon mourned the disappearance of his new bride and assumed she had abandoned him. In time, life went on as usual.

Occasionally, Michelle would venture close to the house at night, but never had to return to her human self. One night she was prowling near the house. She didn't see the gun that killed her. She felt a searing pain and then darkness.

Simon went to his grave without knowing he had killed his bride, and the two large panthers braying into the night were his offspring.

Historical Note

They arrived in 1728, when the port of New Orleans was alive with the hustle and bustle of daily life. Amidst the chaos, a group of young women disembarked from a ship, each clutching a coffin-shaped cassette or casket. These oddly shaped suitcases held all their possessions. After a grueling six-month journey across the Atlantic, they were eager, yet apprehensive, about their new lives in La Nouvelle-Orléans.

Handpicked by the Bishop of Quebec under the French King's orders, these women arrived with one purpose: to marry French colonists in the burgeoning Louisiana colony. However, upon their arrival, whispers spread among the townsfolk. The Frenchmen, noting their pale complexions, muttered "Pâle" as they watched the women, whose skin blistered under the sub-tropical sun.

Known as the Filles à la Cassette, the women were initially placed under the care of the Ursuline nuns. Yet, their fates diverged from the King's plans. Many faced disrespect, forced marriages, or worse, were driven into prostitution. Displeased, the French King ordered their return to France.

To prepare for their departure, the nuns gathered the women's casket-shaped chests and stored them on the convent's third floor. This area had always been sealed, and it remained so. But when the nuns returned, they discovered the chests were empty, and the women had vanished.

Fearing the true nature of the women, the Ursuline nuns took measures to secure the third floor, using nails blessed by the Pope to seal the windows. The whispers in town grew louder, now with one ominous word: vampire. The mystery has survived for over 300 years, but regardless of who or what they were, some of these women were not who they claimed to be. Some were not vampires at all; some were something else entirely.

Lois Curran

Lois Curran is an award-winning author whose work blends gripping suspense with emotional depth. A life-long story teller, she has earned recognition for her compelling characters and tightly woven plots, establishing herself as a rising voice in the mystery and thriller genre.

Born in Arkansas and raised in Oregon, Curran eventually settled in the Ozarks, which she now calls home. Beyond her writing, she is an active leader in the literary community. She serves on the boards of Sleuths' Ink Mystery Writers and Between the Pages Writers Con, and is also a proud member of Ozark Romance Authors, where she helps mentor and support aspiring authors.

When she isn't crafting her next novel, Curran can often be found attending writer conferences, sharing her love for the craft, or capturing moments through her amateur photography. A passionate traveler and cruise enthusiast, she documents her adventures and engages with readers worldwide through social media.

Whether at the gym, on the road, or with a latte in hand at her favorite café, Lois Curran continues to inspire both readers and writers with her dedication, creativity, and storytelling excellence.

Alone and Scared

It was a dark and stormy night.

The wind roared and rattled the shutters, the sound causing gooseflesh to stand erect on Tina's forearms. She hunkered down under a blanket, praying the storm would pass by soon. Lightning zig-zagged through the townhouse making the hallway look eerie. A loud clap of thunder vibrated the window, and she jumped.

Clink.

That sound made every hair on the back of her neck stand up. A palm flew to her mouth. Was someone in her bedroom?

Good grief! Get a grip. How could someone be in here?

Crack!

Not my imagination. Someone is in the other room.

Fear grew claws, and she grabbed her phone. She shot from the sofa and pushed through the front door. She punched in 911, her breath coming in ragged bursts. Rain battered her face, while tears intermingled with the downpour, and she could barely see two feet in front of her.

"911 what is your emergency?" a calm voice asked.

"I think someone is in my townhouse." She rattled off her address.

"Are you in there now?"

"No, in my car."

"Help will be there in five minutes."

A bolt of lightning illuminated a dark figure darting out

of her front door, and she dropped her cell.

Oh my gosh, someone was in my apartment.

But how did they get in? Must have already been there when she got home from work. And that had been over an hour ago. A shiver crawled up her spine, while she cranked the ignition.

Staccato lightning illuminated the sky, splitting the heavens open, while she slammed the gear shift into reverse.

Thump. Thump. Her vehicle only inched backward.

Okay, just get out of the car and see what's going on.

She pushed open the door and her startled breath rushed into her lungs, letting the cold wind enter her entire body. She hugged herself to ward off a chill.

Both back tires were flat. An ice pick protruded from the whitewall on the right one. Rain washed over her and dripped down in splashes around her feet. A hard fist of urgency punched her in the gut, uprooting her, and she threw open the trunk and palmed the tire iron.

Just when her hand found the driver's door handle, she felt a presence behind her. She turned, and a figure dressed in black sweats and a ski mask grabbed her shoulders. A shiver crawled up her spine. *Who is this maniac? And why is he focused on me?*

He grabbed her arm when she twisted to the side and pulled her toward him as easily as if she were a child. Something sharp sliced into her side while the downpour pelted her face. Fear encompassed her, smelling like death.

He's going to kill me.

Suddenly adrenaline soared through her, preparing her body for the fight-or-flight response. She sucked in a breath and swung the tire wrench like her life depended on it.

Her weapon connected, and he buckled but didn't go down. Unbelievable. She'd smacked his kneecap and heard it crack, but there he stood, eyes shooting daggers through that blasted ski mask.

"Nice try," he said.

That voice. I've heard it before. She raised the tire tool again, but he snatched it from her in a split second and threw it to the ground.

"Okay, now you're gonna die."

A deep guttural snicker, barely audible, escaped his throat as a switch flipped on in her memories.

She knew who this fiend was. Jeff Richards, her ex. After six months his open-handed slaps across her face had turned to fists, and she knew she had to escape his abuse. She'd had to get a restraining order to keep him away, and he had sworn he would make her sorry for leaving him.

She'd moved to a gated community after he broke the order and nearly killed her. He had served a year in the county jail after that episode, and she thought he'd given up on his revenge tenacity. Apparently not.

All at once headlights hit her face, blinding her for a second. A police car pulled to a stop and two uniformed officers jumped out, guns drawn.

Jeff tried to run, but thanks to her handy lug wrench, he didn't make it far before the cops grabbed him.

He raised a clenched fist toward one of the policemen.

"Don't even think about it." The officer tapped his Glock. "Now hands behind your back." She watched the man in blue snap handcuffs on her stalker.

"Are you okay, miss?" cop two asked.

"I think so." She placed a hand on her side. "I think he stabbed me."

"An ambulance is on the way," he said and took her arm. "Let's get you in the squad car. You're soaked."

These were the last words she heard before blackness overtook her and she fell forward.

Vengeance is Mine

The air smelled like dead fish and stale water, a mixture that gave James a headache. He felt his clothes starting to become damp from the sweat that pooled over his body. He held the gun, feeling the cold steel underneath his fingers, and dug his nails into the revolver, trying to distract himself somewhat from the pain surging his veins. He shifted the gun from his right hand to his left, tucked it under his belt, and made sure his shirt tail concealed the weapon.

Just then, he spotted him. Bob, who up until yesterday was more like a brother than a lifelong friend.

Your time's up.

He raced toward his prey. He could hear his ragged breaths echo down and come back to him as he huffed forward. A few more long strides and he closed the distance between them.

"Hey, wait up," James called out. "I need to talk to you."

Bob stopped, turned, and James saw the recognition slide across his features.

"Hey, buddy," Bob said. His eyes grew wide. "What's up?"

Bob wore tight western jeans that looked like a second skin. A smirk tugged at his mouth.

Funny how I've never noticed his arrogant persona.

James got right to the point. "What were you doing at the Savings and Loan with my wife?"

"I wasn't *with* her. She was there. I was there. We spoke."

"Don't give me that. I saw you two leave together."

"So? We walked out the door at the same time. No big deal. Don't get your Fruit of the Looms in a wad."

James laughed without mirth. "And I suppose you both just happened to slide into your car. And then accidentally kiss."

Bob's expression changed from smirk to trembling lips. "Okay, buddy. I'm busted. I don't know what I was thinking. But believe me, it meant nothing. It means nothing. Just a few shared kisses in a momentary lapse of judgement."

"You make me want to puke. You're supposed to be my best friend. I trusted you with my life. And what do I get? You go behind my back and mess with my wife. My wife! You could have anyone you wanted. Why did you do that to me?"

"James, I swear, it wasn't planned. It started out as innocent flirting and one thing led to another. I am sorry."

"You've got that right. You are one sorry excuse for a friend. I'm done with you. I'm done with her."

"I never wanted to cause a breakup. This was a stupid move on my part and I regret it."

"How long?"

"A couple weeks, that's all. And it was dying out. For both of us."

"So, if I hadn't caught you guys in the bank, you wouldn't be giving me this *it's over* crap. You two must have had a good laugh at me, huh? Poor ole stupid James. He doesn't have a clue what we're doing. I was such a fool to trust either one of you."

"Aw, don't be like that. This was nothing. I swear…"

James threw up a hand. "Spare me the graphics. Whatever comes out of your mouth now won't fool me again."

James shifted from one foot to the other, and pulled a revolver from the waist of his jeans. He pointed it at the one he used to call friend and watched him run a trembling hand across his forehead peppered with sweat beads.

"Hey, buddy." Bob made a peace sign with two fingers. "Take it easy with that. That's no way to settle anything."

"It's the only way for me."

"No. Come on. Think about it. Let's go to Mary's Tavern, sit down, and have a cold brew and work this out. You know we have always been able to fix anything that got messed up between us."

James laughed. "I don't want to fix anything with you. I want to end something. And that's what I'm going to do. I'm going to put a bullet right between your lying, deceiving eyes. Then I'm gonna take this gun home, wipe my fingerprints off. I've already made plans to take my sweet little unfaithful wife to the shooting range, so she'll have her prints all over this baby." He waved the gun at his ex-friend.

"You are losing it, man…"

"Nope. I'm just getting it together. She's gonna go down for your murder. And guess what, *buddy*? I'll have the last laugh."

The bullet punched its way through Bob's forehead, causing a gaping hole that quickly filled with blood and gushed out.

Rest well my friend.

The Last Passenger

Detective Beverly Anderson hated night shifts at Union Station. The place always smelled faintly of wet concrete and stale coffee, and the late hours brought out shadows that even security cameras couldn't catch.

Still, it was the perfect hunting ground for predators, and that's why she was there.

A week earlier, a young woman named Milly Larson had vanished after boarding the midnight train to Chicago. Surveillance caught her entering Union Station, but no footage ever showed her leaving. Beverly's gut screamed abduction, though the brass had been quick to float theories about runaways and voluntary disappearances. But then another passenger, a middle-aged man, vanished two nights ago. That couldn't be coincidence.

Beverly convinced her captain to let her ride undercover. No backup. No partner. Just her instincts and the Colt tucked under her jacket.

At 11:37 p.m., she bought a ticket from a vending kiosk. Seat 14C. She let her gaze wander, slow and careful, as she moved through the terminal with a faded duffel bag slung over her shoulder. The disguise of a weary traveler.

The concourse wasn't crowded, just a scatter of night owls. A teenager wearing a KC Chiefs sweatshirt dozed on his backpack. A middle-aged woman paced while shouting into her phone. Two men in suits whispering near the newsstand.

And then she saw him.

Tall. Lean. Dark coat too heavy for spring. He leaned against a column, pretending to scroll on his phone, but his eyes flicked often, too often, over the crowd. Not at the departures board, not at the vending machines, but at the passengers themselves.

Predator eyes.

Beverly adjusted her course to angle his reflection into the glass wall of the ticket office. He wasn't looking at her, not yet. His gaze snagged instead on the teenager near the benches, earbuds in, oblivious. The kid was maybe sixteen, a lamb among wolves.

Her pulse quickened. Was this her man?

At 11:55, the gate attendant called for boarding. Beverly moved with the trickle of passengers, her duffel strap biting into her shoulder. She felt the man in the dark coat fall into step several people behind.

The train smelled of oil and metal, the narrow aisle lined with gray cloth seats. She slid into 14C window side, where she had a clear view of both the aisle and the exit doors.

The suspect chose a seat five rows back. Too far for casual interaction, too close to ignore.

She kept her breathing steady, outwardly calm, though every nerve screamed with alertness. At 12:07 a.m., the train shuddered, groaned, and pulled from the station. Darkness swept past the windows as the city shrank behind them.

The first twenty minutes crawled by. Passengers settled. A conductor checked tickets. The steady rhythm of the tracks built a low lull. Beverly forced herself to keep still, her eyes half-lidded, her breathing slow, but every flicker at the edge of her vision spiked her pulse.

Then the man rose. At first it was casual, like stretching his legs, but his gaze swept the car in measured arcs. He moved down the aisle, pausing once to steady himself on a seat. His eyes brushed over Beverly, lingered just long enough to register her, then slid past.

He stopped beside the teenager. Bent low. Whispered something.

The kid shook his head, looked confused, and tugged one earbud out. The man leaned closer, his hand brushing the back of the seat as though to steady himself. But it wasn't steadying. It was claiming.

Beverly stood and stepped forward toward the suspect. "Excuse me. Restroom's this way, right?" Her voice resounded sharp, controlled.

Both heads snapped toward her. The man's eyes narrowed, cold, calculating.

"Back that way," he said, jerking his chin. Smooth voice. Too smooth. The kind that came from rehearsal.

"Thanks." She moved past, brushing close enough to smell him. A faint, sterile tang clung to him like antiseptic. Maybe alcohol wipes. Not cologne. Not sweat. Something clinical.

Instead of heading to the restroom, she lingered just beyond the connector to the next car, keeping herself hidden. Her heart thudded as she peeked back.

The man waited until she was gone. Then he drew something from his pocket. His body shielded most of it, but under the dim light she caught the glint. A syringe.

Her stomach turned.

She slipped her phone out, fingers flying as she typed. **Suspect onboard. Train 627. Male, 6'1, dark coat. Possible syringe. Advise Chicago PD to meet at Union Station.**

No bars. No signal. The message stalled, taunting her.

She cursed under her breath.

He leaned closer to the kid, voice low. Beverly couldn't hear the words, but she saw the teen's posture stiffen, his hand twitch toward the call button on his seat. The man's other hand tightened around the syringe.

Decision time. Wait and risk the boy getting dosed, or move now?

She stepped forward, hand brushing her weapon beneath her jacket. “Sir,” she said evenly. “Step away from him.”

Heads turned. Murmurs rippled. The suspect froze, then straightened slowly. The syringe vanished into his coat pocket with a sleight-of-hand grace that sent chills down her spine.

“You talking to me?” His voice was lazy, mocking.

“Yes. Hands where I can see them.”

The kid ripped his other earbud out, eyes huge.

The man smiled. Thin. Sharp. “Lady, you’re making a scene.”

“I’m a detective.” She flashed her badge. “Hands. Now.”

For a heartbeat she thought he might comply. Then his smile widened, curling too far, like a crack spreading through glass.

And he ran.

The aisle erupted in chaos. Passengers shouted, stumbling back as he shoved through. Beverly lunged after him, her shoulder slamming against a seat. The train rocked beneath her feet, the roar of wheels on rails drowning her shouts.

He tore through the connector to the next car, knocking luggage loose, ducking past startled travelers. Beverly pushed harder, Colt drawn now, her lungs burning.

He slammed through another door, heading toward the rear. The baggage car. Empty. Perfect ground for whatever he planned.

Inside, shadows draped over stacked crates and bicycles strapped to rails. The air was colder here, metallic.

He stood at the far end, chest heaving, syringe gleaming in his hand.

“You should’ve stayed in your seat,” he said. His voice had lost the smooth veneer. Now it was jagged, urgent.

"You don't understand. Nobody listens. They never listen."

"Drop it," Beverly said, gun steady. "It's over."

His eyes burned, fevered. "It's not what you think. They wanted me to do it. They all wanted it. The quiet ones. The ones nobody misses. The city doesn't care about them, so I take them before the city eats them alive. I make it fast. Painless."

Her skin crawled. He wasn't just a predator. He thought he was merciful.

"You murdered them," she said.

"I saved them." His grip tightened on the syringe. "And now you'll ruin it. You'll drag it into the light. But you don't understand, detective. Darkness is kinder."

Then he lunged.

Her finger tightened on the trigger. The gun cracked, deafening in the confined space.

The man staggered, the syringe clattered across the floor. He clutched his chest, mouth opening in a silent gasp, before collapsing against the crates.

Beverly's arms trembled, her ears ringing, but she kept her aim steady until his chest stilled.

For a long moment, the only sound was the rattling of the train, the metallic rhythm of wheels grinding steel. Then, slowly, she lowered her weapon.

Crew members burst in minutes later, the conductor pale. Beverly identified herself, badge flashing under the harsh fluorescents. They called ahead to the authorities. Chicago PD would be waiting, they assured her.

She crouched beside the body, forcing herself to look. He was younger than she expected, early thirties, maybe. A scar carved along his jaw. His pockets gave up two more syringes, each capped and filled with pale liquid. Ketamine, she guessed. Fast-acting, paralyzing.

She thought of Millie Larson. The missing man. Others, maybe, who had disappeared into the night without a ripple. This wasn't random. He'd been hunting. He'd been rehearsing. Perfecting.

When the train screeched into Chicago at dawn, Beverly stepped onto the platform, exhausted but upright. Officers met her and guided her to a remote spot. She relayed everything, every detail precise, facts etched in her mind like scars.

They wheeled his body away under a tarp, faceless now, just another piece of evidence. The officers spoke in clipped tones, assuring her she'd done the right thing. But their voices seemed distant, muffled under the roar of arriving trains and the shuffle of morning commuters.

Normal life surged around her as if nothing had happened. Coffee carts hissed steam, suitcases rattled on tiles, announcements crackled overhead. Strangers hurried past, eyes glazed with the dull weight of routine, not one of them glancing at the blood still drying on her cuffs.

And in that moment, Beverly realized the man had been right about one thing: the city didn't notice the quiet ones. Didn't notice the vanishings. Didn't notice the dark until it bled out in gunpowder and screams. Millie Larson and the others, they had been invisible until she dragged their killer into the light.

But what if he hadn't been the only one?

She thought of the antiseptic tang on his coat, of the precision in his movements, of how calmly he'd carried the syringes. He hadn't been sloppy, hadn't been reckless. He had been practiced. Groomed. Maybe trained.

Her chest tightened as the thought rooted deeper.

What if Union Station wasn't just his hunting ground, but his assignment? What if he was only one among others, scattered like shadows across the country, plucking passengers from the edges of the map where nobody would look too hard?

She forced herself to breathe, to walk, to hand over her weapon for evidence processing. But the ringing in her ears didn't fade. Neither did his last words.

Darkness is kinder.

That phrase whispered against her skin as she moved through the station, past faces she would never remember, faces that could vanish tomorrow without notice. Maybe he had been delusional, a madman cloaking brutality with self-justification. But maybe he'd been telling a sliver of truth, too. A truth colder than the dawn air cutting through the terminal.

Because as Beverly glanced at the crowd, she saw him again. Not his face, not his body, the man was zipped into a black bag, but the echo of him in every dark coat, every lingering gaze, every commuter with eyes that shifted too fast.

For the first time in her career, Beverly wasn't sure if she had ended something or only stumbled into its beginning.

The train pulled away behind her with a long, low groan. She watched the steel snake vanish into the horizon, its cars rattling like bones. The sound followed her out of the station, into daylight that felt thin, weak, incapable of pushing back the shadows pooling in her mind.

She had stopped one predator. But she walked away with the cold certainty another would step off a platform tonight, syringe in his pocket, smile in the dark, waiting for the next quiet soul the city would never miss.

M.E. Rowe

M.E. Rowe is an award-winning fiction author who dabbles in multiple genres, but her true love lies in suspense. Growing up on Scooby Doo, Stephen King, and Unsolved Mysteries fostered her desire to delve into the darkest places of the heart, mind, and soul.

She resides on ten secluded acres in Southwest Missouri with her beloved husband of too many years to count, two spoiled rescue dogs, and one incredibly sassy calico.

Thick as Thieves

The robin sounded from the clock above the mantle, signaling one a.m. I'd always complained that clock was loud enough to wake the dead, but tonight I prayed it wasn't loud enough to wake the living.

My mother had always been a heavy sleeper, but I couldn't afford to get caught sneaking out tonight. Creeping from the couch to the window, I silently popped the screen out of the frame for the first time in nearly fifteen years.

Once outside, I headed to the wellhouse. My eyes filled with tears as I pulled the backpack from the brick structure. Our wellhouse was the place I met Kate when we snuck out to do dumb, reckless teenage things our parents would never allow.

Focus, Josey-girl!

I proceeded down the familiar, now overgrown, path through the woods separating my mother's house from the Mackenzie's. Technically, it was the Kyger's. Mr. Mackenzie's daughter and son-in-law, Kate and Jack Kyger, lived there now. Growing up, Kate Mackenzie was my neighbor and best friend. We were inseparable, practically sisters. Thick as thieves, our parents used to say.

Concealed by trees, I watched for any signs of life. The flicker of a television was the only light. Jack Kyger was likely passed out in front of the TV. I was counting on it.

Hardly the image of stealth, I darted across their yard. Then my gloved hand hovered over the garage doorknob. If the door didn't open, the plan was cancelled. I almost hoped the door wouldn't open.

Kate was always the brave one when we were children. She didn't take crap from anyone. She was my rock when my dad died. She nursed me through breakups and all the other losses in life.

During our sophomore year, Kate dated Jack Kyger, the most popular guy in our school. A few dates turned into an invitation to his senior prom, then they were officially a couple. Jack was jealous and controlling from the beginning. After they got together, I saw less and less of the fiery Kate I'd always known.

Jack peaked in high school. He dropped out of college, going to work for his father's dealership. Jack was relegated to detailing cars until he knocked up Kate during her senior year. It was okay to make your son pull himself up by the bootstraps when he flunked out of college, but a grandchild promoted you to Sales Manager.

Kate and Jack married right after our graduation. I tried to talk her out of it, but nothing could sway her devotion to him.

Jack was too macho to be in the delivery room for the birth of their son, so it was me coaching and holding Kate's hand through labor. I was the first one to hold their son, Jaxson. Despite Jack's DNA, Jaxson was perfect.

Kate and I remained close through the years despite Jack's disapproval. Whenever I visited, Jack would plan things for Kate to do while I kept the baby. When Jaxson was school age, he stayed with me for a few weeks every summer while his parents took a couple's vacation. Jaxson and I were close, and I cherished my visits with him.

Their family dynamic became clearer over time. Jack was a functional alcoholic, barely coasting by at work. They moved into Kate's dad's house right after Mr.

Mackenzie died because their house was in foreclosure. They always drove new cars belonging to the dealership, not to them. Kate and Jaxson got an allowance from Jack's parents to keep them nicely dressed because they knew Jack mismanaged money, and appearances were important.

After years of begging, pleading, and cajoling, Kate decided to leave Jack but unfortunately, she waited a little too long.

Kate called me late one afternoon, hysterical. "Jaxson didn't go to school this morning, he ran away! Has he called you?" I assured her I'd tell her if I'd heard from him. Kate bawled. "He's been missing almost twenty-four hours!" That didn't make sense, he'd only been missing since that morning, when he didn't show up for class.

When questioned, Kate admitted she and Jack fought the night before, that he knocked her unconscious. Jaxson was home then, but she didn't check on him when she came to. He was gone when she went to wake him for school. His backpack was gone so she thought he left early, that he didn't want to face her after last night. When the school called a few hours later reporting Jaxson's absence, Kate immediately called Jack, who hadn't seen Jaxson since dinner the night before.

Kate said she searched the house for clues. Jaxson's Nintendo Switch was gone but the charger and games were left behind. His secret stash of cash was missing but he didn't take her stash of cash. I stopped her. "Your stash of cash?"

Kate divulged she planned on leaving Jack. She'd been taking money from his wallet and saved part of each allowance from her in-laws to build some savings. She was waiting for Jaxson to turn twelve next month because she was advised that was the youngest age a court might take into consideration which parent a child wants to live with after a divorce. She didn't tell Jaxson they were leaving, it might put him in danger if Jack found out, but she did show him where she kept her money in case anything ever happened and he needed it. Kate believed Jaxson ran away to get away from Jack and left her money behind so she could do the same.

Kate broke down again, "Jaxson left to make me rescue myself, now he's missing and it's all my fault!" I reassured her everything would be okay, but I was wrong.

Once I got back to Missouri, I searched with the volunteers and spent all my free time with Kate. We talked about everything. I learned the awful details of her marriage; there were photos of injuries and recordings of threats Jack made that she could use for leverage to leave safely. She really was planning to leave Jack.

There was no sign of Jaxson for a week. Nobody suggested he might never be found, but the search party volunteers dropped exponentially each day. Kate clung to the hope Jaxson was waiting her out, waiting to know she left Jack, before he resurfaced. My grip on that hope was more tenuous. Jaxson was eleven, he didn't have the resources to wait her out. But I agreed to her plan to come to Colorado with me in a couple of weeks if Jaxson didn't show up, to flush him out of hiding.

I returned home to Colorado to get ready for Kate. Two days before I was supposed to leave to get her, I was shaken awake, Kate's voice whispering, "Wake up, Josey-girl, there's a change in plans."

I was shocked to see her in my room, in my house, in Colorado. I was even more shocked by her appearance. The kaleidoscope of bruises on her face and neck stood out starkly in contrast to her pale, fair skin. We talked for hours, crying and scheming, before she left. I wouldn't see her again until we met in her garage.

When Jack called to tell me Kate was missing, he thought she was depressed about Jaxson running away and might have hurt herself. I told him I hadn't heard from Kate since I left Missouri, but I'd be there tomorrow to help look for her. Jack told me it wasn't necessary, but I insisted. I was headed home anyway, but Jack didn't know that.

Focus, Josey-girl!

I twisted the doorknob, heard the quiet snick of the latch releasing. Kate's bruised but beautiful face waiting in the doorway reinforced my resolve. Kate watched approvingly as I opened the gun safe with the combination she provided, watched my hands shake as I loaded almost every chamber of the revolver, the same revolver Jack pointed at her countless times to play his sick game of Russian Roulette.

Once the weapon was loaded, I opened the backpack and geared up. One of my mom's old plastic shower caps and a pair of my dad's old fishing waders really complimented my dingy old sports bra and my purple nitrile double-gloved hands.

Kate giggled, commenting it looked like I had a bread bag on my head. I gave her a caustic look, asking if she'd prefer to do this alone. She smiled politely and bowed, directing me toward the kitchen. She was right on my heels as I entered the house. The stench of rotten food and dirty dishes assaulted me but didn't deter me from grabbing the notebook with the pencil stuffed in the silver spiral off the counter before stepping into the den, Jack's Man Cave.

Jack didn't stir as we approached. I kicked the raised footrest, startling him awake. Alcohol-fogged confusion cleared once he saw the revolver. "Hey Josey. What's going on? Why don't you put that down, let's talk. We can figure out where Kate is."

I aimed the revolver, commanding, "Sit back and shut up!" He smirked but remained seated as I continued, "I'm talking and you're listening." The smirk evaporated. I was uncertain if that was because of my words or that he just realized why I was dressed this way.

Nervously, he said, "Hey now, Josey-girl, I don't know what you think—"

I cut him off, snarling, "I'm not your Josey-girl! And I don't *think* anything, I *know*. I know everything, and you're going to tell everyone else or I'm going to make you pay!" I stepped closer with the pistol to drive home the truth of what I was saying. "Kate told me everything, you bastard. I saw the bruises on her throat!"

Jack's face was ashen as he murmured, "She told… Her throat? You saw her throat?"

I screamed, "You beat her unconscious. Jaxson tried to stop you and you killed him, your own son! And when Kate figured it out, you killed her too!" I threw Jaxson's spiral notebook in Jack's lap, ordering him to write down what he did, where to find them. Jack stared dumbly at me so I fired the gun.

I saw urine spread across his lap as he flinched, preparing for impact., but it was the empty chamber. When his eyes met mine, I told him I knew about his Russian Roulette games with Kate, adding, "But I play differently, only one empty chamber instead of five. Now write!"

He hesitated, looking up to ask, "How did you know?"

Sighing warily, without a believable explanation to give, I truthfully said, "Kate told me. Her, Jaxson, everything. You know we're close, thick as thieves, our parents used to say."

Jack scribbled furiously then thrust the notebook toward me. "Here! Is this enough for you to call the police now?"

I did it
Jaxson and Kate
Blue Eye
I'm sorry
Jack Edward Kyger

I read his words then retorted, "I'm not calling the police. Somebody will, eventually, I'm sure. But, yes, I think this is enough for everyone to know what a piece of shit you are. You didn't deserve Kate. Or Jaxson. And they didn't deserve anything you put them through!"

Jack wasn't looking at me anymore. His horrified eyes were fixed on something behind me. I followed his line of sight.

"Jaxson?" My voice trembled as I took in the ghastly sight. Bloated, discolored, and waxy skin not sitting exactly as it should, I still knew it was Jaxson by the shock of blond hair.

"Hi, Auntie Josey."

I stared, confused. Jaxson looked exactly like you'd expect for being submerged in water for a month. Each time I saw Kate over the last week, she still looked like I assumed she did when Jack choked her to death, but before he threw her in the quarry with Jaxson.

Kate! I scanned the room and saw her standing in the corner looking at Jaxson with a mixture of horror and sorrow. This was the first time she'd seen him since he disappeared. My heart broke even more as I saw Jaxson smile at her. The corners of his lips split and some of his teeth fell out, scattering across the hardwood floor.

Heartbreak swiftly became fury. I swung around to Jack, who was transfixed by the monstrous visage of the son he murdered and dropped into Blue Eye, the old quarry we used to swim in as teenagers. Making Jack's death look like suicide was over. I didn't think I could stop at just one bullet. I was going to empty this gun on him, consequences be damned!

Before I could pull the trigger, I felt a cold, clammy hand on my forearm, forcing the gun away. Jaxson softly said, "You can't do this, Auntie Josey."

I sputtered, "I... I can!"

Sweetly, Jaxson said, "No, you can't become what he is. You're going to hand him the gun and he's going to do the right thing, aren't you, *Dad*?"

Jack feebly nodded in agreement. Hesitantly, I stepped toward Jack, unsure if I could hand over the gun, to trust he wouldn't use it on me.

Jaxson coaxed, "It's okay, I promise." Whether Jaxson was a ghost or a figment of my imagination, I believed him. I handed the revolver to Jack, who took it with steady hands, and without hesitation, pulled the trigger.

Ears ringing, I swallowed the bile that rose in my throat at the gory scene of blood, brain, and bone. I turned around to see Kate and Jaxson hugging, now looking as they had in life, perfect in every way.

Kate pulled away from Jaxson, still holding his hand, "Josey-girl, there's work to do. Nobody can know you were here."

Back in the garage. I changed back into my regular clothes and packed the backpack. I left the gun safe open, exiting the way I entered.

Kate and I held Jaxson's hands as we walked through the woods toward my mother's property. We discussed the possibilities of how they returned to their pre-death images, how Kate came to me as soon as she died but why Jaxson couldn't communicate with us until Jack admitted what he did. And what happens next.

With no conclusions reached, our conversation organically ended as we approached the other side of the woods. I stuffed the backpack inside the wellhouse before I noticed they weren't with me.

Kate and Jaxson were standing at the edge of the woods, holding hands, expressions pained. I walked toward them, uneasiness rising.

Kate spoke, "I think this is it, Josey-girl. We can't go any further with you."

Jaxson added, "But we'll always be with you."

Then together, "Thank you. Love you, Josey-girl." They vanished before I could reach them.

Awestruck, I stared into the woods, waiting for… something. The calling sound of the wren told me it was four a.m. My soul felt light as I climbed back inside the window.

Sharon Kizziah-Holmes

From her musical roots to her success as an author and entrepreneur, Sharon embodies the spirit of creativity and determination in the heart of the Ozarks.

In the 1990s, Sharon and her husband made the move to the beautiful Ozark Mountains. A talented musician by trade, Sharon continued to perform, but a new passion began to blossom: writing fiction.

Sharon's journey took an exciting turn when she joined Ozarks Romance Authors. This opened doors to new opportunities, including attending conferences and workshops. Immersing herself in the writing community, she honed her skills in both writing and navigating the dynamics of publishing.

Her dedication and hard work have resulted in a collection of **twenty-one published titles**! Her writing spans a diverse range of genres, including:

- Historical Westerns
- Contemporary Romance
- Contemporary Western Romance
- Mystery
- Short Stories
- Children's Books

Driven by a desire to support fellow writers, Sharon established Paperback Press, an indie author service company. She finds great joy in sharing her knowledge and expertise with aspiring authors, guiding them through the often-complex world of writing and publishing.

Today, Sharon continues to live in the Ozarks with her husband and their two dogs, Willie and Waylon.

Royalty Statement

Joanna Peach was getting frustrated with her sister. "Diane, pull your weight. I feel like I'm dragging him all by myself."

"Hey, it was your idea to bring him into the woods to bury him. Don't gripe or I'll turn your ass in."

Ohhh, she didn't just say that. "If you do, you'll be turning yourself in as an accomplice. I wouldn't be the only one to go to jail."

"I'd get a lighter sentence for cooperating."

"You wish." Trying to catch her breath, Joanna stopped and let her side of the body bag drop on the ground. "I think this is far enough."

"Good." Diana let the shovels and her part of the body bag go. "Let's get this over with."

"Yes, I'm ready to put his royalty stealing carcass six feet under." It was hard to believe she had killed her publisher and had actually talked her sister into helping her get rid of the body. The ass was a thief! She'd written seven full-length mystery novels and wondered why she didn't have much money coming in, in royalties. Her ratings were good, so she knew she was selling books.

"Six feet! Bullshit. I'm not digging a hole that deep."

She rolled her eyes. "It was a figure of speech, Diane. Damn." She picked up her shovel and started to dig. The dirt was hard, and it was cold out. Mid-winter, when the ground was frozen, wasn't the best time to try to bury a dead guy. She was tempted just to take the body out of the bag and let it rot on the ground. It would give the animals something to feast on. No, that was out of the question.

"Jojo?"

They'd only been digging five minutes and already her older sister was out of breath. So was she, for that matter, but they couldn't stop. "Yeah, Di."

"How much money do you think this bastard stole from you? I mean, is it really enough for you to have done this?"

Laughter crept up her throat and out her mouth. "Now's a good time to be asking that question. The deed is done. And besides, you mean *was* it enough."

"Was? What are you talking about?"

She'd been suspicious for quite some time and thankfully one of her good friends worked for the small, traditional publishing company. Her friend happened to be a writer, too. She'd also had doubts he was being honest with royalty payments. The two of them decided to delve a little deeper.

Once they got to the real royalty statements, and compared them to what was paid out, shit hit the fan, but only she had gone back after hours and taken her revenge.

"One night when I knew he was going to be there late, I stopped by the office. I convinced him I wouldn't shoot him if he gave me the money I had coming. In cash! That SOB just happened to have it in the safe at the office. He handed me $223,000 dollars!" Sweat was rolling off her brow now. The cold air didn't do anything to stop it, but she kept digging.

"No shit? $223,000?"

She stopped, leaned on the shovel handle then smiled. "Welllll…it may not have been quite that much, but that's what was in the safe." When her sister stopped digging, she met her gaze. "See, once he opened the safe, I held the gun on him and went to the doorway. I'd hidden the body bag just outside. I got it, made him get in it, and put two pillows under his head. Once I zipped it up. I pulled the trigger. The pillows absorbed the blood. I took the money and here we are. By the way, I'm giving you $50,000."

"I'll take it, and you're a genius."

"Why, thank you, ma'am." She gauged the length and depth of the hole. "I think this is big enough. Let's throw him in, then put some dirt on top. We'll put the shovels on top of that and fill the rest of the hole in by hand."

"Sounds like a winner."

When they were done, Joanna handed her sister the $50,000 she told her she'd give her. "Quite the payment for a half day's work, huh, sis?" She joined in with Diane's laughter.

"You got that right. Anyone else in mind you want to whack?"

"From now on, only in my novels. However, now I have to find a new publisher."

Eye Witness

"Th-that guy has a gun!" Jacqueline barely got the words out before the gunshot rang in her ears. She watched the man with the weapon turn and run. The expression on his face frightened her as she watched him exit. Her feet were frozen in place. The voices of her co-workers seemed miles away.

"…ambulance…"

"…911…"

"…after him…"

"…Jack's the only eyewitness…"

Her world faded to black…

The scene before her slowly came back into focus. How did she end up sitting in an office chair? She put her hand to her head hoping the room would stop spinning. What the hell just happened?

She stood on shaky legs and made her way to the circle of people. Her heart jumped to her throat and bile rose from deep within. She swallowed hard and inched closer. Her boss lay motionless on the cold, hard tile, his eyes…empty of expression. Blood seeped from the wound in his chest and puddled on the floor beneath him. Then she remembered the man with the gun.

She glanced at the door where she'd seen him enter, shoot, then leave. His face forever etched in her mind.

The tarmac sent up clear, rippled waves of heat as Jacqueline peered out the airplane window. Before they started to travel, the flight attendant gave last-minute safety tips.

They were now in the air, and she was happy to get away from Dallas. She was a bonified Texan, but the heat of summer was exhausting, as were the reoccurring nightmares she couldn't shake. Her personal paradise was exactly what she needed to get over the tragedy she'd witnessed. Three months alone was her ticket back to sanity. The sweet smell of Alaska's spring wildflowers would make her forget the face that haunted her.

The secluded cabin her uncle left her near Seward was in the wilderness. She'd come here every summer since his death. Wildlife and beauty surrounded the cozy cabin, and one neighbor whom she loved. Angelia was tough as nails and had lived in the backwoods of Alaska all her life.

She smiled remembering the first time she'd met the rough, tough, dark-skinned woman.

"Why, honey? You're gonna have to get those hands dirty if you want to survive around here. I bet your uncle Homer didn't even tell you how to load or shoot a gun."

"A gun. Why would I need a gun?"

"You never know when a bear might wander up to the cabin and break a window trying to get in."

She'd never thought of that, but it made perfect sense. She was alone in the Alaskan outback. Thanks to her friend, she now knew how to load, fire, and clean a pistol and a rifle.

It was great to see Angelia and her pearly white smile waiting by the general store. "Well, it's about time you got to town, Jack. I've been waitin' all of fifteen minutes. Surprise! I took the liberty of getting you some supplies."

"You're a peach." She gave the older woman a hug. "Thank you for taking care of me."

"Never you mind about that." Angelia led the way to her all-terrain vehicle, her Great Pyrenees dog in tow.

"What would I do without you, Ang."

"Why, I imagine you'd survive."

The sun dipped behind the trees as they pulled into the driveway. She wanted to get inside and lay down. It had been a long trip and jet lag was setting in.

"You know if you need anything, Angelia's here for ya, right?"

"I know, and I appreciate it. Right now, I'm going to bed."

Angelia left, and darkness engulfed the cabin, at the same time blissful sleep overtook Jacqueline.

She startled awake. Was that a gunshot? A dog barked outside. She grabbed her gun and opened the door. Angelia stood over a man on the ground, a pistol in his hand.

"Ang, what's going on?"

She pointed to her dog. "Man Man was acting weird, so I thought I'd see why. I found this man pointing his gun at you through the open window. I hollered and gave him a chance to put the gun down, but he turned and pointed it at me. I did what I had to, to survive.

When Jacqueline looked at the man's face her heart jumped to her throat. "It's him!"

"You know this guy?"

"No, I-he killed my boss a few months ago." She glanced at her friend. "We've got to get rid of the body."

Miss Killer Crawford

"Hi, could you point me in the direction of the police station?"

Sara stepped off the curb and wondered why the 'new guy in town' needed the police. She'd seen him earlier in the week at work. Apparently, he was the new vice principal at the elementary school where she'd been head librarian for the past three years. "Is everything okay?" It wasn't any of her business, but she hoped nothing serious was wrong.

"Aren't you Miss Langley?"

They hadn't met formally, yet he knew her name. "Yes, and you're Alan Brendon."

"I know."

"What?" Boy, up close he was hot!

"That I'm Mr. Brendon."

He had a smart ass sense of humor to go with his good looks. "Funny guy."

"Thanks. Police station?"

She pointed north. "If you take the next right, go to the red light, make a left, it's on the right side of the street. Hope everything works out okay with…whatever." Obviously, he wasn't going to tell her what happened. Again, it was none of her business.

"Thanks." He smiled. "Oh, and something's a little cockeyed, but probably nothing to worry about. I noticed some weird goings on around my new place and wanted to alert the authorities. Maybe they'll patrol the area more frequently."

Her heart skipped a beat. Hadn't he bought the old Crawford place? He should probably call an exorcist. Weird was a tame word for the 'goings on' around there. She wasn't going to tell him he bought a house considered the most haunted in the midwest. She'd let the police be the ones to inform him about the crazy lady who was man crazy. Besides, he should have done his research. "Well, I hope you figure it out."

A horn honked but Alan didn't seem to hear it. Sara turned to see a strange woman looking at herself in her rear-view mirror. She was dressed like someone from the 1950s and the car was a model from the same era. Strange. The woman glared at her, honked again, then focused on Alan's car.

"Come on, my love, get movin'. I have someplace to be, but she's not expecting me."

What the hell did that mean? My love? Could Brendon be her boyfriend? No, surely not. She stepped back onto the curb. "Bye now." She watched Alan's vehicle go out of sight, then turned toward the woman's car. Wait, where'd it go? Where did *she* go?

Sara swallowed hard then glanced up and down the street. There was no sign of the woman or her car...anywhere. Okay, maybe she imagined the whole thing. Thinking about hauntings, plus Alan's good looks had her mind in a whirl.

She needed a hot bath. At home, she filled the tub and got in. Someone's hand pushed on her head. She glanced up. The woman in the car! Ghost white, she wore a wicked smile, her voice, haunting.

"Alan has eyes for you, but he bought my house so he *will* be mine…Once you're dead, bitch."

J.C. Crumpton

JC Crumpton was born in Southern California and grew up in San Diego, Chicago, Iceland, Germany, and Arkansas. He lives in Northwest Arkansas with his wife, his cat, and her dog.

Chief Carter: Marooned

Something woke him. Not a sound. Something less tangible. Keeping his eyes closed, he listened to the noises of the pod. The recycler struggled but didn't struggle any more than it had when he went to sleep. He heard Firth snoring like someone rubbing fine sandpaper over a smooth block. Occasionally, the computer whirled up to speed, probably calculating some scan result.

He didn't hear Damon. The kid always breathed through his mouth. He told Carter he had narrow nasal passages but never bothered getting the operation to fix it. All the ribbing about being a mouth-breather never bothered him.

He squinted his eyes against the light, rolling his head over. The young sailor wasn't in his seat. Nor was he anywhere Carter could see. Sticking out from the wall like a lump of dirty laundry, the lieutenant commander slept.

Movement at the left edge of his vision drew his gaze. A single glob of red liquid hung suspended in the air, drifting in the slight currents. He'd seen blood balled up in zero-G before. His eyes shifted around the pod. Only the sleeping officer and the missing sailor were out of place.

He released his straps and pulled himself across the compartment to Firth. Searching the man without touching him, Carter didn't see any scratches or bruising. His knuckles were free of abrasions, and he had no blood on his jumpsuit. The left pocket, half turned under him, bulged from its contents. The man's pockets were empty the last he saw.

Carter leaned in closer and tapped the man on the shoulder. His breathing stuttered. His eyes blinked rapidly. He jerked upright, his arms lashing out to the side.

"What're you doing, Chief?"

Not answering him, Carter stared at the officer. He took in a slow deep breath, letting it fill his lungs. The stale air and Firth's pungent body odor stung his nose.

"Is there something you want to tell me, sir?"

The man breathed soft and quick. His brow wrinkled, and a drop of sweat beaded in the furrow and sat there, growing. His face screwed up like he was holding back tears.

"He volunteered, Chief. I swear it."

Beeps sounded from the computer. The officer shifted his attention between the chief and the empty console. Carter didn't look away. He waited, his mouth in a tight line.

"What did he volunteer for, sir?"

Without meeting his gaze, the lieutenant commander answered, "To save us."

"How did he do that, sir? We are secure here. No enemy. No life-threatening malfunction. There is enough air. There is enough food."

Shaking his head back and forth, tears welled up in the corner of Firth's eyes. The moisture flung into the pod, floating until splashing against the hull.

"It wouldn't have lasted long enough."

"Long enough for what?"

"Until rescue."

"How do you know?"

The computer beeped again, its drive whirring to life. Firth blinked.

"You said it could take six weeks. Maybe longer."

Carter nodded. "We had enough rations for six weeks."

"At half rations." The officer whimpered.

"We needed to be strong for Bedford, sir. He was a kid."

Firth pushed his jaw out, sniffing. "He volunteered. If we get picked up, I will recommend him for the Navy Cross."

The chief scratched the side of his nose. "He can have mine."

The other man's eyes widened. He looked behind Carter when the computer started beeping.

The lieutenant commander whispered, "He volunteered."

"A brave act. Needless and unnecessary. But brave."

Carter pushed away from the officer, gliding over to his side of the compartment. The computer beeps stopped, and he looked at the monitor. Something with a Navy identification code was reaching out into the system with aggressive and active scans.

"Hmm." He sat back in his seat and stared across the pod.

Firth turned away, frowning. Carter could tell the man wanted to ask what was on the monitor by the way his eyes darted over to him but shifted the other way if the Chief looked back.

"Would you like to know what long range scans are telling me, sir?"

The other man continued to stare at the ceiling. Carter knew the officer's curiosity would eat at him. He waited, glancing over at the monitor and mumbling something incoherent. His fingers drummed against the overhead compartment.

The officer started to sweat more, and until he swiped the back of his hand and sent the droplets flying, they beaded up like silver warts sprouting across his forehead. Tears filled the edges of his eyes.

He raised his head. "He volunteered, Chief. I will be vindicated and charge you with insubordination."

Carter smiled. "Not this time."

Twisting around in his seat, he started pecking on the

keyboard below the monitor. He opened the internal hard drive, expanding the folders until he reached the file he wanted. Internal CCTV.

"What is that, Chief?" There was a tremor in the lieutenant commander's voice. He wiped at his forehead.

Shrugging, Carter dropped the files into the permanent memory banks. This sub-system could not be altered from the ship itself. He tapped the icon for the folder starting at 0200.

He pulled the monitor out and turned it so Firth could see it from across the compartment. The first scene showed the interior of the escape pod. Carter watched himself sleeping, strapped down with his hands crossed over his chest. He looked drained. Bedford sat in his seat, reclined back but with the monitor pulled over so he could see it.

On the monitor, the lieutenant commander hugged his knees to his chest and squinched his eyes, watching the young sailor. His eyes didn't waver. Carter could tell Bedford was getting tired. He cursed under his breath. He made a mistake when he set the kid on watch.

As soon as Bedford's eyes closed, the officer released his own straps. He pushed off and drifted across the compartment. Bedford didn't move. His mouth open, breathing deep and regular. Every now and then, moisture droplets would launch from his lips and float until being picked up by the ventilation.

Carter glanced at the clock on the video. Ten minutes before 0300. He wouldn’t wake up for another three hours. The lieutenant commander grabbed the rings above Bedford's seat, arresting his momentum and allowing his legs to swing to the floor.

Reaching into his left pocket, he pulled out something small enough to hide in the palm of his hand. On the screen, Firth looked over his shoulder. The chief turned his head, staring at the officer and shaking his head. Back on the monitor, Bedford cleared his throat and repositioned himself as well as he could.

Firth turned his head back around. He knelt down, coming up under the steel arm holding the monitor. Something glinted in his left hand. Carter paused the playback and enhanced the image. A telescoping screwdriver. After pressing it against Bedford's temple, he stepped back and waited. The kid opened his eyes, blinked twice, and swallowed.

Seconds rolled over on the clock. Two minutes had passed before Firth pulled himself back to the sailor. He reached out and put his hand against the kid's nose. Nodding, he collapsed the screwdriver and tucked it into his pocket.

On the screen, Firth carried Bedford's body over to the airlock and dumped it in like a bag of trash. Carter felt his anger rising. Heat crept up his neck. His heart pumped, the blood rushing through his head and pounding in his ears. He watched Firth secure the inner door and reach over. He hit the yellow button first, letting the ship systems cycle the air out of the airlock. When he hit the green button, he didn't even bother to look at Bedford's corpse blown out into the void.

The time stopped at 0259. The images went blank. Carter caught the reflection in the screen, as Firth launched himself across the compartment. He cursed. He should have expected the officer to try to get rid of him as well.

Carter pressed off against the hull and closed the distance. Firth jammed the screwdriver into the chief's right shoulder. The pain made him grunt. The impact spun them around.

Reaching up, Carter held his hand over Firth's as it gripped the handle. The officer tugged at his hand instead of attacking Carter's eyes or face, trying to get away. Carter pulled his legs to his chest and then stretched them out to wrap around the officer's hips. Firth struggled, his voice shrieking as he tried to get free.

Tangled together, the two men drifted toward the top of the pod. Firth could not see the hull coming up behind him and tried to wrestle free. Moments before they struck the hull, Carter took his left hand off Firth's. The lieutenant commander grinned. Carter pushed with his left palm and bounced the officer's head off the hull. The chief kicked out with his feet, propelling the two men back across the pod to the floor.

Carter twisted them in the air and tucked himself into a ball. His body drove into the lieutenant commander hard, forcing him to expel all his air. Ribs cracked, and the officer barked a sharp cry. Rolling off, Carter grabbed rungs at the base of the hull next to the floor. He halted his movement and watched as Firth bounced off the floor, ricocheting toward the top of the compartment.

The man's body shook with sobs. His cries echoed through the pod. Carter narrowed his eyes. If you can't handle the pressure, stay on the surface, he always thought. He took the officer and hauled him over to the man's seat. He took a few straps from one of the lockers and restrained Firth in place.

Carter went over and tapped a few icons on the monitor. A view of the system's white dwarf glared on the screen until the computer automatically dimmed it.

"You see right there?" Carter pointed to an orange flare forty-five degrees to the sun. "That's the Confidence on its way to pick us up. It'll be here in two days."

Firth whimpered. "I didn't know."

"Now you do."

"I can't move, Chief."

Shrugging, Carter settled into his seat before pushing the monitor back into its bay on the hull. "Neither can Bedford."

"What if I have to use the restroom?"

Carter smiled. "I'm not going to hold your hand. Mess your pants."

"Chief!" Firth started thrashing against his bindings and screaming. "Let me out of here. That is an order."

Reaching over to the monitor, Carter tapped a couple of icons. The ventilation shut down. He cut the oxygen mix to a lower percentage. Firth started to gasp, trying to suck in more and more air with each inhalation. After thirty seconds, his head lolled back, and his jaw fell slack. Carter could feel a headache coming on, so he tapped on the screen until he restored full flow and the right oxygen mix.

After sending the CCTV files to the Confidence, he strapped himself in and settled back to wait for the rendezvous. Sleep came in fits and moments. Firth had to be knocked out three times before he learned not to push his luck. The rest of the wait, he glared at Carter in silence.

The pod shuddered as it slipped into the Confidence's hangar bay. Firth's face went white. His breath whistled through his nose, and Carter thought he might start hyperventilating. But though his color never returned, the officer stayed conscious, even when the MPs came on board and escorted him onto the ship in restraints.

One of the welcoming committee stayed behind with the two corpsmen checking Carter over, making sure he didn't have any internal injuries. The officer, standing still in his dress whites, waited. Both corpsmen wore decontamination suits and informed him he would still have to undergo quarantine.

Carter smiled and climbed on the gurney. "Let's go."

Exactly the Same, Just Different

Jaden stepped off the shuttle, pushing his pack higher up as he stepped down the ramp. This New Ankara looked no different than all the other backwater outposts he had visited. Everyone ran. And they always ran to these out-of-the-way places with hopes no one would ever think to look for them among the flotsam and jetsam of the galactic arm.

Every job started and ended the same—someone with questionable ties to the United Earth government asked him to track someone else who may or may not be a criminal and bring them to justice. Jaden never stayed around to see what happened to the men and women he brought in. Even though he was more accurate with the pulse rifle than the pistol, everyone always told him they had never seen anyone faster on the draw. His skills earned him money that spent. He did what he could to keep afloat in an economy that had become medieval since interstellar travel had opened the universe two centuries ago.

This part of New Ankara received only a few inches of rain each year—and that usually came at the end of summer. The rest of the planet suffered from unpredictable weather, often scouring the land bare beneath winds that blew harder and faster than any hurricane on Earth. Jaden understood why only one percent of the planet's population lived anywhere other than the port town. It would make this job easier. Now he had to come to this forsaken planet because some self-important executive had taken off with important technological schematics the company felt he didn't own. He never questioned ownership because to him the person paying his bills possessed the strongest claim.

Jaden looked out over the brown and yellow plains spreading out from New Ankara's port town. A few dips and rises broke up the monotony, and he watched a storm in the distance while it blew up dust and debris as it raged toward the town. He hoped he could find this Mace Hudgins and get back off the planet before the storm hit and the authorities temporarily closed down any travel.

Good research alleviated a lot of leg work, and Mace had a daughter. The daughter owned a bar a few blocks from the spaceport, a watering hole frequented by enough locals to be self-sufficient but not so many it popped up on must-see places on the Network. People milled about on the street, talking hurriedly and glancing every now and then at the storm clouds building an ugly black scar on the horizon. Some of them nodded at him as he passed, looking first at the patch on his jumpsuit then back at his face before hovering on the holstered gun at his hip.

He turned another corner and stood in front of an adobe building made from the local orange clay. The swinging doors on its front made him believe Abigail Hudgins had watched too many documentaries on the exploration of Earth's North American frontier. Customers packed the place, drinking their fill before the storm hit and shut the town down.

Coming through the doors, a bull of a man barreling out into the street forced Jaden to step back out of the way. The man's round, swollen cheeks flushed red, and a sheen of sweat beaded up on his bald head. His puffy-fingered hands ran back and forth over his naked scalp as he squinted up at the doorway.

"And don't come back until you can settle your tab, Mr. Sweeney," a voice called from beyond the threshold. The discarded patron's shoulders slumped, and he turned away down the street.

Jaden grinned. The voice had been soft in spite of its volume. He wondered why such an angelic voice would be bothered with such trivial words. A voice like that should have people working for it back in the Central Imperium. Not rousting unruly customers from their libations and sullen attitudes.

The inside of the establishment matched the outside. Round tables—not a single one without a drinking customer or two—lay in a haphazard pattern around the room. A stairway to the left climbed up to a walkway that wound around the bar. A long brass rail anchored on the floor in front of the bar where patrons could rest their feet. Exactly the same as all the other bars he'd come across in the Imperium.

Behind the red stained bar, Abigail stood watching him as he entered. She nodded and smiled when their eyes met, her right brow arching just enough that he noticed. Her blonde hair and smooth complexion looked out of place in the dusty town. Jaden swallowed the lump in his throat. He knew from pictures, she was going to be a good-looking woman, only he hadn't been prepared for how beautiful. Maybe it had something to do with how long he'd been skating the back alleys and rarely traveled pathways of the Imperium.

"What can I get for you?" she asked as he dropped his pack on the bar.

He looked at the shelves behind her, but kept returning to stare in her deep green eyes. "Hello," he said. "How are you?" he asked.

Abigail shrugged. "Have to get everyone liquored up before the storms hit."

"I see," Jaden said. He looked around. "I just came in from the port."

She bobbed her head at his pack where he had set it

down with a thump. "I see that."

Jaden smiled. "Obvious, wasn't it?"

"A little." Abigail returned the smile. "What would you like?"

"How about a vodka cranberry with no fruit?"

She nodded. "Can do. But I don't know if you noticed, this place isn't that famous for its abundance of fruit."

"That wasn't a grove of Chinotto oranges I passed on my way here?"

The woman chuckled but didn't smile as she reached under the bar and pulled up a glass bottle with silver script instead of a label. "Koren good for you?"

He arched his eyebrows. "Didn't expect to see something like that all the way out here."

"Well?" She twisted off the cap before grabbing a short, broad-rimmed glass from the shelf against the wall behind the bar.

"Sure." Jaden grinned. "I can afford it."

"I figured," she said, tipping the bottle over and pouring. The clear liquid slipped into the glass almost like oil, thicker than water but thinner than syrup. Maybe it was just an illusion caused by the way she poured it. She added a few splashes of cranberry juice and slid the glass over to him.

He picked it up and let some slide into his mouth and down his throat. The heat slipped along his chest and settled into his stomach just below his ribs.

The glass clinked when he set the glass on the bar. "Mm. That was nice."

"Glad you liked it," Abigail said. She put the cap on the bottle and twisted it tight before sliding it beneath the counter.

The lights in the main room flared brighter, compensating for the shaded light sweeping through the streets. Wind picked up, and the few people out on the street lowered their heads and walked faster.

He took the glass and sipped the drink casually, watching pieces of litter tumble down the street outside the bar. A loud clap of thunder burst near the town and shook the entire bar, causing him to jump and nearly drop his drink. Everyone in the bar stopped talking and looked outside at the darkening sky. Dirty rain, filled with the dust blown up by the storm, splashed through the swinging doors onto the bar floor.

"The storm's moving in faster than I thought it would," Jaden pointed out. "I was hoping to be done with my business and gone before it hit."

Abigail nodded. "Yep. A lot of people underestimate this place." She wiped a rag across the bar top, drying up the moisture ring left by his glass. "What brings you so far from the Central Imperium?"

"What makes you think I'm from the Central worlds?" He licked a droplet off his bottom lip.

The bartender grinned as she wiped a rag across the bar top. "Most people out here don't wear the starburst."

Jaden glanced at the Imperium emblem on his chest, the gold pattern standing out like a beacon on his chest. He frowned. Stupid of him. These backwoods simpletons didn't look on citizens of the Central Imperium as the harbingers of civilization. Any kind of association with the government of the core worlds automatically put him at a disadvantage. Maybe he wouldn't get off planet before the storm.

"Not been my best trip."

"Day's still young," Abigail said.

Many of the patrons scattered around the bar watched the weather rage outside. If storms were a feature of the planet and these people stood around staring out the windows, this one must be special.

He reached over and held his fingers against the glass, feeling the cold from the ice. His throat constricted as he swallowed, but he didn't lift the vodka to his lips.

"How'd you end up out here?"

She tossed the rag into a sink at the end of the bar. "My father set me up with this place."

The ice shifted in his glass. "Awfully nice of him."

"It was."

A hitch in her voice caused him to look back at her. She held a pulse rifle leveled at his chest. He reached for his pistol. He managed to pull it clear of the holster, but he wasn't that fast.

The energy pulse tore through his chest, knocking him to the floor. His vision narrowed, and the light grew dim. He saw Abigail standing above him, an almost-regretful look in her eyes.

"Just different," he gasped. The woman reached down and brushed his hair back from his eyes before closing them.

Zero Mountain

José didn't care. He only needed to be the last one to run. No one knew the truth about what happened. Everyone told a different story each time they told it. According to some, no one ever lived in the house. Others believed several families once called it home until something horrible happened to them and no one ever saw them again. Or something terrifying drove them out.

"Can you do it?" Phillip asked him.

José snorted. "I can do anything you pansies can do. Only better."

Michael barked a quick laugh and punched him on the side of the arm. "You wish. You ever been up there?"

He shook his head. "Never even heard of it."

"Then why do you think you can outlast us?" Phillip asked. "This place is for real, my friend. Scary as all get out. I lasted all of five minutes the first time I came up here."

"Seriously?"

Phillip nodded. "I give you six minutes. This being your first time."

"A whole six?" José said.

His friend shrugged. "I'm giving you six 'cause I think you're pretty tough. You'll stay just long enough to beat my first time. But nothing more than that."

"You shouldn't be so generous."

José looked out the front window. The yellow headlights

chased the night away from the car. They followed the dirt road up and around the hill. Trees with dried brown leaves clinging to the branches closed in on them from either side. He hadn't seen any yard or house lights for a while. Something this remote shouldn't be so close to Fayetteville.

Phillip told him a serial killer lived in the house during the sixties. Supposedly, the man died after a standoff with the local and state police and the FBI. The coroner dug twenty-seven bullets out of the man's chest. Michael believed a cult holed up in the house back in '79. One of their attempts to raise a demon backfired. Authorities found damage to the house in every room. What they didn't find were the bodies of the cultists. Of course, José thought it all crap. They wanted to ramp up his anxiety levels to see if he'd bolt early.

That wasn't going to happen. Six minutes, hell. He decided the ultimate goal would be one hour. Enough time it would end all this talk of serial killers and otherworldly phenomena. He didn't buy into any of it. It was probably an old house creaking on its foundation because of the wind or the frame contracting due to cooling after the sun went down. Any number of real-world explanations. The problem he faced was convincing these fools he wasn't afraid.

Michael tapped him on the shoulder, and he twisted around. "It's up ahead. You really need to see the whole thing to get a real appreciation for it." His friend leaned back against the seat. "I'm telling you. You haven't experienced anything like this."

José shook his head and rolled his eyes. "I bet. Let's get this over with so we can catch the midnight showing of Lord of Darkness."

"Suit yourself," Michael said. "You can't say I didn't warn you."

The car came out of the lane into a large clearing. Phillip turned the car to the right. The yellow beams flashed across a dilapidated, two-story house with a porch stretching across the entire front and back and down one side. Broken glass hung from the window frames like sharp, jagged teeth. They pulled up beside the house, and Phillip turned the engine off.

"You cowards ready for this?"

"Sure," José said. "Still not buying your tales of boogeymen though."

"You will soon enough," Michael said as he opened the back door. "I can't wait to hear you calling for your mama."

José pushed his door open and got out. The others followed, and he pushed it closed behind him. Gravel crunched under his heels.

Calling for his mama? His family descended from Enrique Velarde. He'd show them what bravery meant.

"Let's get to it," he said and walked around the front of the car. "Let this be your lesson in what it means to be brave."

"That's what I'm talking about." Michael drummed his hands over the roof of the car.

They climbed up the three steps onto the porch. Paint peeled off the wooden boards in tiny flecks. Phillip put three flashlights on the window sill by the front door.

"You so scared you need lights?" José asked.

"Heck, yeah, I'm scared," Phillip said. "These are for after."

"Sure." José shrugged and leaned over to peer into the house.

Phillip rested his hand on the door frame. "Some quick rules first."

"You're joking, right?"

Michael chuckled. "Zero Mountain has history."

"Then let's quit messing around and get to it," José said. He glanced back and forth between his friends. "What're the rules?"

“Rule one,” Phillip said, lifting his index finger. “You cannot look behind you at any point. Rule two. Your time is up if you take a step away from your spot.”

“That’s it?”

“That’s it.” Michael twisted the doorknob and pushed. The door creaked on rusty hinges as it swept open.

José followed his friends into the front room. Light from the parked car bled through tattered curtains. A ragged mattress with half its stuffing ripped out and scattered across the floor lay tucked under the window. Other than that, the room was bare. A long hall led away from the door, reaching into the dark depths. José squinted and made out some stairs at the other end.

Phillip nodded down the hallway. “You need to stand at the bottom step. Face the front of the house.”

“That’s it?” José snorted.

“I wouldn’t be too cocky, if I were you,” Michael said.

“I got this.”

José walked down the hall, his feet crunching against grit and debris. The air smelled musty and damp like the locker room at school. He wrinkled his nose. Wind whirled around the house, screeching between cracks in the glass. When he reached the bottom of the stairs, he turned and faced back down the hall.

This must be what the view from the bottom of a well looks like.

He studied the shabby walls, jagged holes in the plaster revealing broken slats. Not drywall like he expected. His gaze shifted up into the open air above him. At least he assumed an open space loomed over him. None of the light from the front of the house could pierce the gloom. The stairwell must reach to the ceiling above because his breath sounded hollow and constricted like he breathed into a long cave passageway.

Something skittered across the wall up the stairs. His legs twitched. He wanted to turn and catch Phillip or

Michael trying to sneak up behind him, but he remembered the rules.

The boards on the upper landing creaked and moaned like a great weight had settled onto it. His heart pounded a quick rhythm against his chest. The pulse in his temple surged. He closed his eyes but snapped them open when something dropped onto the top step. His breath grew ragged, coming in short bursts. He lifted his shoulders, trying to expand his lungs. Nothing helped. He tried to yawn but still couldn't get enough air.

His stomach cramped, and he bent over clutching at his side, grimacing. Sweat popped up across his forehead, running down in front of his temple and stinging the corners of his eyes. The fingers of his right hand quivered uncontrollably, scraping across his thigh.

Something chittered above his head. He took a quick breath and squeezed his eyes shut. The second step creaked. It had to be one of his friends. A burp rumbled up his throat. He tasted boiled eggs moments before the smell of sulfur filled his nose. His lips quivered, and goosebumps rose across the backs of his arms.

Another step. His right knee buckled, and he nearly tumbled over. He looked up the hall. He could no longer see the walls. A thick, black darkness covered everything except for the front door. It hung open enough he could see the headlights. But nothing reached down the hall.

The door swung open. Two silhouettes stood in the frame.

"You beat our time, dude." Phillip's voice cracked.

"Run!" Michael shouted. "Let's get out of here."

"Hurry."

The stairs creaked behind him. He sprinted down the corridor, his feet pounding against the floor. Darkness crept across the doorway. Everything grew dimmer. His friends backed out of the house. Their voices jumbled against each other.

"Run."

"Get out here."

"Faster."

His throat burned. He felt like his eyes were closing. No matter how wide he opened them, the darkness thickened.

"Hurry."

He reached for the door. Something wound around his ankle and jerked his legs.

"No."

He slid back down the hall. Splinters and gravel tore at his flesh. The door slammed shut. All the lights snapped out.

Lynn Combs

Lynn Combs is an award-winning, internationally selling author whose global upbringing as a Navy brat sparked a lifelong passion for storytelling inspired by diverse cultures and adventure. Now based in Southwest Missouri, she writes across genres—including children's books, YA fantasy, and cozy mysteries—and is active in local writing groups and conferences. Her debut picture book, Duncan the Dragon Finds His Fire, marks the beginning of her journey toward a full-time career as an author and speaker. Learn more at lynncombs.com.

Echoes in the Locker

James had heard the whispers long before stepping foot inside Emerson Middle School—stories traded like forbidden secrets, meant to rattle incoming seventh graders. Ghost stories. Items appearing in lockers. Voices in the walls. He hadn't believed a word of it.

Seven weeks into the school year, nothing strange had happened.

Until that Friday.

James lingered late after soccer practice, running extra footwork drills. Sore and sweaty, he decided to take the shortcut through the old wing. It was roped off for renovations—technically off-limits—but it was the fastest way from the gym to his locker.

The corridor stretched ahead like a tunnel into nowhere. Lights flickered and buzzed overhead, casting jagged shadows that seemed to crawl along the cracked tile floor. Rows of tall, dented gray lockers stood like soldiers long abandoned, their paint chipped, vents rusted into grins. These were the full-height lockers, relics from decades ago, nothing like the squat half-lockers that now resided in the rest of the school.

Every squeak of his sneakers bounced back at him, magnified until the sound became sharp, almost human—like a scream.

He was about to turn back when he heard it.

"Help me." A whisper, soft as breath.

James froze. Silence pressed down on him, thick and heavy, as if the hallway itself was holding its breath. His pulse hammered in his ears. He spun around. Nothing. No one.

"Who's there?" His voice cracked, breaking the silence like glass.

No reply.

Then—just for an instant—light flickered from behind the vents of a locker. A glow, gone as quickly as it appeared. He stepped closer. It was the only locker with a dial still attached. Deep scratches clawed across the number plate, but he could still make out the numbers: 237.

James stared, his chest tight. The air around it felt… wrong. Too still. Too cold. Like the locker itself was watching him.

He reached out. Before his fingers touched the dial, it spun. By itself. Right. Left. Right.

Click.

James flinched. His throat went dry, but curiosity overpowered fear. He gripped the latch. The metal burned with warmth beneath his hand. Slowly, the door creaked open, groaning like something waking from a long sleep.

Inside sat three objects:

A worn leather notebook.

A broken wristwatch, hands forever frozen at 3:17.

A curling photograph.

The boy in the photo had a stiff, uncertain smile. On the back, faded but readable: Benji H. 1983.

Tucked in the notebook was a brittle scrap of paper, ink smudged almost to nothing. Two words clung stubbornly to the page: Help me.

James shoved everything back inside, slammed the door, and staggered backward, chest heaving. Then he ran, sneakers pounding the tiles until the hallway stopped echoing his flight.

That night, sleep never came.

James sat hunched over his laptop, digging through scanned yearbooks on the historical society's website. Seventh grade, 1983—there he was. Benji Henderson. The boy in the photo. He was pale and thin with stringy black hair. His eyes were sad and dark.

Something was wrong. The class photo included him, but nothing else did. No clubs. No teams. No other records. It was as if he'd been erased.

And in the back pages—usually crammed with doodles and signatures—someone had scrawled in blocky letters:

'HE WAS HERE, AND THEN HE WASN'T.'

James dug deeper—obscure blogs, archived newspapers, forgotten ghost forums. Finally, on an old ghost-hunting subreddit, he found this:

The message appears every October 13th, in locker 237. 'Help me.' Happens like clockwork. The faculty try to hide it, but kids whisper about a ghost.

Friday, October 13th, the exact date listed in a decades-old article: the day Benji Henderson disappeared.

James's fingers shook as he texted his best friend, Derek:

James: meet @ 6am 2mrow, usual spot
Derek: 2 early
James: OMG be there
Derek: k

The next morning, James spilled everything.

"You found a haunted locker?" Derek grinned. "Cool."

"I'm serious," James snapped. "That kid—Benji—he disappeared. There's no record of him after that year. And the message shows up every October 13th. Same day."

Derek's grin faltered. "Every year? That's… messed up."

Together, they slipped into the old wing. Locker 237 loomed, the air around it charged, humming faintly like static before a storm.

"Go on. Open it," Derek urged.

"Don't rush me," James said as he slowly reached for the dial. Again, it spun on its own. Right. Left. Right. Click.

The door creaked open. The same three items sat waiting inside, undisturbed.

"This is officially creepy," Derek muttered.

James pulled the items out when footsteps echoed suddenly, sharp and heavy. James slammed the locker shut, heart pounding.

"Who's there?"

The voice was gravelly, unmistakable—Janitor Bob. He was always lurking, watching.

They ran for the next hallway headed away from Janitor Bob's voice. They made it around the corner just in time. They leaned against the wall and froze, lungs burning with the effort to quiet their breath.

They heard metal clanging against metal, followed by a curse. "Dang locker gets harder to open every year."

James and Derek exchanged a wide-eyed look. A sudden bang rang through the corridor, making them jump. They bolted, sneakers slapping against the tiles as they fled, taking the long way to their lockers.

Over the next days, their investigation deepened.

James buried himself in the school archive room, while Derek combed through the downtown library. Dusty papers. Forgotten files. Whispered warnings.

A week later they got together to share notes.

"In 1989," Derek said, "Students heard crying in the gym showers. No one there. In 1997, yearbook staff ran out screaming after finding 'Please don't leave me' scratched into the floor."

James added, "In 2005, a teacher had a panic attack during detention—said voices whispered from an empty corner. And in 2013, the AV Club filmed a project. Static laced with a child's voice: 'Still here.' The file was deleted…"

"I found a copy posted on the internet," Derek interrupted, pulling out his phone. With a few taps he had the shaky video playing. Together, they leaned in, listening to the faint, desperate whisper. "Still here."

James shivered as they looked at each other wide eyed.

Every incident circled one date: October 13th. The day Benji vanished.

Thirteen disturbances in forty years.

The deeper they dug, the darker it grew. A retired teacher confessed in an interview:

"He was a quiet boy. Got picked on. Always carried a comic book. Then one day… he didn't come back from lunch. Police said he ran away. But that didn't seem right."

From there, the truth only grew stranger, more dangerous.

And it all came back to Locker 237.

They tried several times to return to the locker, but Janitor Bob lingered in the wing too often, his heavy boots echoing down the halls like a warning. His eyes always seemed to catch theirs, sharp and suspicious.

"It all centers on that locker," James whispered one afternoon. "We need a closer look."

"Yeah, but when? How?" Derek asked.

"It's gotta be soon. Construction starts Monday. Once they rip the place apart, we lose everything."

Derek grinned, the reckless kind of grin James hated. "Then we stay. Overnight."

James blinked. “What?”

“Tomorrow’s Friday. We say we’re at each other’s houses, hide after practice, wait for everyone to leave.”

“That’s insane.”

“Got a better idea?”

“No…, but…”

“Do you want to know what happened or not?”

James swallowed hard. “Of course I do.”

“Well then…”

James sighed. “I guess we go for it.”

The next day they stashed flashlights and snacks in their lockers. Each class dragged on like molasses, nerves jangling with every bell.

That night, they slipped into the gym equipment room, crouching among dusty mats and racks of balls until the school went still. Once they were sure everyone had left for the weekend, they crept out.

The old wing was darker at night, suffocatingly so. The air carried a tang of mildew and something faintly metallic, like old blood. Locker 237 loomed in the beam of James’s flashlight, paint peeling in curls that looked like dead skin.

It opened just as before, as if waiting.

“I don’t see anything,” Derek whispered, sweeping his light.

“Wait—the screws.” James crouched. “Three are missing on the back panel.”

“So?”

“If you angle it… look—it slides hinging on this one top screw.”

With a rusty screech, the panel shifted, revealing a narrow vent. The stench of rot rolled out, dry and heavy, like a tomb exhaling.

James, smaller than Derek, swallowed his fear and

wriggled inside, past the back panel and into the wall behind it. His flashlight beam caught a blanket, stiff with age, a rusted thermos, and a comic book cover curling with damp. Then the light hit bones.

He froze.

Pale, brittle, unmistakable. Bones.

Heart hammering, James pushed aside the blanket. A lunchbox sat tucked against the wall. Inside, it was empty except for a faded library card that bore the name: Benji Henderson.

“He was here,” James whispered hoarsely. “And no one ever found him.”

Before he could back out, the panel slammed shut. Metal clanged. He was trapped.

“Help!” His voice cracked with panic.

“I got it!” Derek grunted, sliding it open again. James scrambled free, gasping.

“That’s what happened,” James said, his voice hollow. “He got stuck and it was a Friday night. He was alone in there, all weekend.”

Then the air shifted.

A glow seeped from the vent, soft at first, then brighter—like moonlight bleeding through cracks. A figure emerged. Thin. Frail. Transparent.

Benji.

“You found me.” His voice trembled, layered with echoes. “I was so scared. I kept waiting. But no one came.”

James’s throat tightened. “I’m sorry.”

Benji’s hollow eyes lifted. “Can I go now?”

James nodded.

A small smile ghosted across Benji’s face before he dissolved into smoke, fading like breath in winter air.

“We have to let the police know.”

“Yeah.”

It should have ended there.

A week later at school, Derek shoved a newspaper at James. “We’re famous!” The headline praised them for uncovering Benji’s fate.

“Yeah. And we got fan mail,” James muttered, sliding an envelope from his locker.

Inside, jagged handwriting scrawled:

He’s been found, now leave it alone.

Don’t go digging around where you don’t belong!

Derek paled. “Someone’s watching us.”

“Not just watching,” James said. “Warning. Benji was in that locker for a reason. The world needs to know why.”

“Agreed,” Derek added.

The boys interviewed a former classmate, Jessica Andrews, who revealed three names. Three boys who had bullied Benji all the time:

Tom Jenson, now a lawyer and school board member.

Rick Taylor, owner of Taylor Construction, the company renovating the school.

Bob Sorenson. Also known as Janitor Bob.

Jessica added, “Cops searched Benji’s locker and his home, but nothing was ever found. They said he ran away. But that didn’t seem right. I felt sorry for him and should have helped him, but I was afraid of what my friends would think.”

Soon after, the threats escalated. Derek’s bike tires were slashed. James’s locker was broken into—his notes and Benji’s photo gone.

They couldn’t get close to Tom Jenson or Rick Taylor. But Janitor Bob? He was right there.

They began to follow him. They observed that he spent a lot of time down in the boiler room.

“That’s our next place to look,” James whispered.

“Right.”

The next morning, they arrived before school and crept down to the boiler room. It was suffocating—hot pipes rattled, steam filled the air like a sauna. Shadows writhed across the walls, the smell of oil and ash clinging to their throats.

Behind a loose grate, they found everything: James's stolen notes, Benji's photo… and dozens of scraps of paper scrawled with the same desperate plea: Help me.

A brittle paper lay tucked beneath them. An insurance policy, a confession.

We, Tom Jenson, Rick Taylor, and Bob Sorenson, swear to never tell anyone what we did. Each of us will keep a signed copy of this note outlining our part in Benji's disappearance. We all stick together, or we all go down together.

James's hands shook. "They made a pact not to say anything. They thought the truth would stay buried. But they were wrong."

The words had barely left his mouth when a voice snarled behind them.

"What're you kids doing down here?"

The boys jumped, turned and ended up face to face with Janitor Bob.

James straightened, defiant. "We know what you did."

Bob's eyes narrowed. "Should've burned those papers years ago. But now? You'll never leave with them."

He lunged. Derek dodged, but Bob's fist clamped around James's arm like iron.

"You think you're heroes?" Bob growled. "You don't know the trouble you've stirred up. You should have left the past in the past."

James struggled. "Benji knows. And now everyone else will too."

Then suddenly the air changed.

The pipes shrieked. Lights flickered—then burst with sharp pops. The temperature plummeted. Steam hissed, filling the room with a choking mist. Shadows swirled, stretching long fingers along the walls.

From the fog, a shape emerged. Pale. Hollow-eyed. Radiating cold.

Benji.

"You left me."

Bob staggered, grip loosening. "No…"

"You locked the door," Benji's voice boomed, echoing through pipes and vents.

"We thought—you'd be fine—"

"You laughed. You left. You lied."

Words bloomed across the misty walls in dripping letters: Help Me.

Bob's knees buckled. "It was… just a joke!"

Benji's translucent gaze turned to James and Derek. "Run!"

The furnace groaned. Tools clattered from hooks. The boys bolted, the door slamming behind them as if pushed by invisible hands.

They didn't stop until they reached the principal's office, blurting everything in gasps. Police swarmed the school within hours.

Janitor Bob was dragged from the boiler room, trembling and babbling incoherently. Tom Jenson and Rick Taylor were arrested soon after. The town knew the truth at last.

Weeks later after the renovations were finished, the school held a memorial. Benji's parents attended. They couldn't thank the boys enough for finding the truth.

During the dedication service, Benji's parents stood teary-eyed as Principal Santos announced: "Locker 237 will be welded shut. A plaque will be placed in his memory."

The polished metal door now bore the words:

In memory of Benji Henderson.

May the silence never return.

Every day, James passed it. The hallway stayed quiet. But sometimes—when the hall was empty, the lights flickering just so—he still heard it. A whisper, soft as breath.

"Thank you."

The Sassy, Sexy, Senior Sleuth's Society

A dark and stormy night, perfect weather for the society's meeting, Agnus thought as she adjusted her pearls in the hall mirror. She did so with the same determination she once used to put on her nursing gloves before delivering babies. Tonight required the same sense of ceremony.

Hilda had called earlier, announcing she was bringing her visiting nephew, Nick—a real-life New York police detective. Agnus could already imagine it: their little club elevated with an air of realism. After all, what sleuth society didn't need a skeptical lawman to roll his eyes at them?

The doorbell rang. Thunder rumbled overhead, rattling the glass panes.

"Perfect timing," Agnus muttered as she opened the door to a swirl of wind, wet umbrellas, and the familiar chorus of chatter.

She took hats, coats, and umbrellas with military precision, piling them onto the hall rack that leaned precariously from years of abuse. Nick trailed in behind his aunt, looking like he'd just walked into an episode of *The Golden Girls*.

Once everyone was seated in the parlor, Agnus clapped her hands for order. "After Irene's excursion to an actual crime scene last week—" She paused for dramatic effect. "To which I must add, wonderful sleuthing, girls! The police would have never solved it without us."

The members shared knowing nods and murmured agreement, except Nick, who raised an eyebrow so high it nearly touched his hairline. Agnus could have sworn she heard him mutter "busy bodies" under his breath, but she was not about to let a little muttering ruin her thunder.

"Ladies, ladies, please, let me continue." She puffed up like a hen about to lay a prize-winning egg. "I thought long and hard about how to top last week's society meeting, and I believe I've done it!"

Right on cue, a crack of thunder shook the room. Irene shrieked, knocking over her glass of sweet tea, which Hilda saved with a reflexive snatch. Agnus smiled—her flair for timing was unmatched.

"I've created a murder mystery right here in my kitchen, and you're all going to solve it!"

The women burst into applause, fans flapping, pearls rattling, lipstick-smudged grins shining with delight. Nick did not clap.

Agnus continued, "Now ladies, your job is to discover, who he is, how he was murdered, who did it, and why."

She led the way to the kitchen, skirts swishing, while Nick followed like a man heading to the gallows.

The moment the women spotted the body on the kitchen floor, they surged past Agnus as if it were a Black Friday sale at Macy's. They clustered around the corpse with squeals and sharp commentary.

"Look at that reddish tint to his skin," Hilda pointed with her cane. "He must have been poisoned, most likely arsenic."

"He has an indent in his ring finger but no ring. He must be married," Mabel observed, already squatting low like an arthritic Sherlock.

"Or trying to hide it," Irene countered, peering over her spectacles.

"Or divorced," Hilda added.

"Or robbed!" Mabel declared.

"Or dead," Nick muttered rolling his eyes and ignored by all.

Mabel, not to be outdone, started unbuttoning the corpse's shirt. "Several stab wounds! Oh, the drama."

Irene produced a blacklight from her oversized purse like a magician pulling a rabbit from a hat. "I always carry it for hotel rooms." She flicked it on, bathing the body in a ghastly purple glow.

"You can see bruising around some stabs but not others," Hilda noted. "I wonder if more than one person stabbed him."

"Move it back up to his face—I think I saw something!" Hilda directed.

The beam shifted.

"A handprint on his cheek! I'll bet he was slapped," Irene crowed, far too pleased.

Meanwhile, Hilda was wrist-deep in his pockets. "I found his wallet! His name was Calvin Silas."

In the dining room, Nick helped himself to some of the snacks laid out on the table and muttered, "Good-looking fake body. I expected something more like what you would find at a Halloween-store."

"That wouldn't be realistic," Agnus sniffed, arranging deviled eggs.

"How'd you get it in here?"

"I dragged him in through the kitchen door, and he's not fake," she replied matter-of-factly.

Nick choked on a cookie. "What!?" He bolted into the kitchen. The ladies barely noticed as he put his arm around Hilda's middle to lift her out of the way and set her down behind him.

"Nicolas! That's no way to treat your auntie," she huffed, slapping his arm.

He reached for Irene.

"I've had both hips replaced," Irene added, batting his

hand away. "You can't just fling me like a sack of potatoes."

"Sorry, ma'am," Nick muttered. "But I need you all to step aside and stop touching the body!"

Mabel yanked out a crumpled note from beneath the body squealing, "I found something!"

"Leave it where it is," Nick demanded.

"It's a note…" She read it aloud in a dramatic whisper:

Calvin,

You lied for the last time...

The ladies gasped like a synchronized choir. Nick tried not to scream. Mabel continued…

and I'm not the only one you have lied to. I know about the others. I make you one final vow. You will never lie or cheat on anyone ever again!

Nick decided to use the distraction to kneel and examine the body on the floor. "This is a real body!" he exclaimed.

"I told you," Agnus said, folding her arms. "You can't have a murder without a body."

Nick dragged his hands down his face. "Who is he? What happened? How did he get here?"

"That's what we're solving, dearie," Agnus replied sweetly. She leaned toward Hilda. "Is your nephew a bit slow?"

"Must be the city smog," Hilda whispered back.

"I'm going to have to insist you all stop touching everything!" Nick commanded a bit more forcefully than he had intended.

Hilda walked over to Nick patting him gently on the shoulder. "We have to examine it to solve the crime."

"No! We need to stop touching everything and call the police!"

"Nonsense, that's the role you are playing tonight," Agnus said.

"This isn't my jurisdiction."

"That's okay, it's just for fun."

"Murder is fun!"

"Well, real murder is terrible, of course. But this is fun."

"This is a real murder! Did you kill him?"

"No, I only stabbed him."

"What?" Nick nearly fainted.

Agnus sighed as she explained, "He was already dead. I just stabbed him."

"You stabbed a dead body?"

"Of course.

"Why would you do such a thing?"

"He said he would help me out and be our corpse in tonight's mystery," Agnus explained.

The mystery temporarily forgotten, everyone turned and watched the exchange between Nick and Agnus.

"There is nothing to get upset over, dearie. This is my neighbor," Agnus continued.

"And his name is Calvin Silas?"

"No. He's playing Calvin. His real name is Burt. He promised to be our corpse, but he died this afternoon."

"How?"

"He had a bad heart. So, I'd say a heart attack."

Irene interjected, "Agnus would know, she's a retired nurse."

"Plus, everybody knows Burt always keeps his promises, no matter what," Hilda added.

"Exactly," Agnus said. "He wouldn't want something like his death to get in the way of keeping a promise. Since he no longer needed his body, I was able to add a stabbing instead of old Burt just pretending to be poisoned."

"A much better scenario, for sure." Irene clapped her hands together.

Nick turned back to Agnus. "So, then what?"

"I brought him here, cleaned him up, washed his clothes—he was rather sweaty and dirty after working in his garden in the hot sun. Then I redressed him, stabbed him, poured some homemade fake blood around the wound and placed the clues."

"Well done on the blood," Mabel said.

"Thank you," Agnus replied. "It's just a bit of corn syrup and food coloring, but it did turn out nice, didn't it?"

"Oh, yes." Irene answered.

"Ladies please, let's stick to the facts." Nick ran his hands through his hair.

Hilda put a reassuring arm around her nephew. "Nick, honey, there is nothing to be upset over."

Nick pulled his phone out of his pocket. "I am calling 911 and getting the local authorities here."

"There's no need. I was going to call Fred, the coroner, to pick up old Burt after we finished our mystery," Agnus said. "It's all fine."

Nick didn't reply. He was on the phone with the 911 operator. After disconnecting he insisted everyone leave the kitchen until the authorities arrived despite several objections.

With a sigh, Agnus suggested they all enjoy the refreshments and discuss the clues they had found so far until the Sherrif arrived.

Before long there was a knock at the door. Agnus opened it to Sam. "Howdy Sherrif, come on in. Would you like a bite to eat?"

"You know I can't resist your cookin'," Sam said. "But I reckon I should take a look at Burt first."

Agnus led the way to the kitchen and Sam knelt over Burt. He put his hand to his neck and declared him dead.

"Well, Agnus, looks like his heart gave out. Burt always did work too hard in that garden. You ladies go on and finish your mystery, I'll call Fred to pick him up later."

Nick sprang to his feet. "That's not police procedure!"

Sam sauntered into the dining room and started making a plate of food for himself "Son, let me tell you this… Unlike your big city, things are done differently in small towns like ours. Everyone knows everyone. Agnus has been a nurse and midwife in these parts for over fifty years. She started out as a teen helping her mama do the very same thing. If Agnus said Burt died because of his bad heart, then you can bet the farm on it. I'll have an autopsy done, of course, but I'm sure ol' Fred will find that it was just as Agnus said. So, there is no need to pull Fred away from his dinner and deny these ladies their murder mystery fun. I am sure it is what old Burt would have wanted. Now sit down and let the ladies play."

The society cheered and rushed back to the body, nearly knocking Nick over as they swarmed the poor man again like bargain hunters at a yard sale.

Nick started to pace, trying to make sense of it all.

Suddenly Irene shouted, "I've solved it!" fanning herself with her notebook as though she were Poirot at a garden party.

All eyes turned to her. She straightened her brooch and cleared her throat with theatrical gravity.

"Calvin has been bed-hopping with at least two mistresses. His wife found out and confronted them. They both swore they didn't know he was married. So—naturally—his wife poisoned his food with arsenic, then invited the mistresses over so they could stab him to finish the job!" She flourished her hands as if unveiling a grand stroke of genius.

Everyone applauded, waving their lace handkerchiefs and clapping their manicured nails together in delight.

Except Nick.

He slumped into a nearby chair, gripping his temples. "You've got to be kidding me…" he muttered.

But Irene wasn't done. "The slap on the cheek? That was the wife's final insult—because nothing says betrayal like a good slap before poisoning stew."

"Yes, yes!" Hilda crowed. "I knew I saw lipstick smudge on his collar. Scarlet Passion Red, to be exact. One of the two hussy's he has been running around with must have left it there!"

"Wait," Mabel interrupted, digging in her handbag. "I have a magnifying glass—ah ha!" She leaned over the body, squinting through the glass so close she nearly toppled forward. "Yes! You can clearly see where another woman tugged at his shirt. That's proof of mistress number two."

Agnus beamed like a proud mother hen. "Ladies, this is some of our best work yet."

Nick groaned and tugged at his tie. "This isn't work. This is… chaos."

Hilda ignored him. "But what if the wife didn't do it? What if all three women formed a pact, poisoning him together? A revenge sorority!"

"That's brilliant!" Irene declared. "A secret club of betrayed lovers—like our sleuth's society, but with more knives."

The women erupted into cheers at the thought.

Nick buried his face in his hands. "What kind of Twilight Zone hell did I walk into?"

"Careful, dear," Agnus said, patting his arm. "You'll give yourself wrinkles with all that frowning. Have a cookie. It helps with nerves."

Nick waved her away, muttering something about "evidence contamination" and "career-ending reports," but nobody paid him any attention.

The ladies had returned to the corpse, debating loudly whether the stab wounds were evenly spaced (Mabel swore one mistress had shorter arms and therefore the angle was different), while Irene insisted the arsenic must have come from Calvin's favorite lemon pie, noting the custard stain on his shirt.

The room filled with clapping, theorizing, and the crinkle of candy wrappers as the sheriff raided the snack table again.

Nick leaned back in the chair, staring blankly at the

ceiling fan spinning overhead.

He was a decorated NYPD detective. He had solved murders in alleys, kidnappings in warehouses, even a jewel heist in Central Park.

But nothing—nothing—had prepared him for Agnus, Hilda, Mabel, Irene, and a dead man named Burt who kept his promises.

For the first time in his career, Nick had no idea what the crime was, who the suspects were, or why the sheriff was currently sipping sweet tea and asking for seconds on deviled eggs.

He was certain of only one thing: He would never accept another invitation from Aunt Hilda again.

When the Mist Comes

It's been twenty-five years since my wife and I opened this bed-and-breakfast. By daylight, it looks like any other quaint house in the hills: white clapboard walls, blue shutters, flower boxes spilling over with color, and a porch that creaks underfoot like it remembers every step that has ever crossed it. Sometimes I think it sighs at night, as though it knows what waits beyond.

But when the sun dips behind the ridges, and the shadows stretch long across the garden, the hills breathe differently. The wind slows. The trees stand too still. Even the stars seem to hesitate, holding their distance, as though they know what waits below.

Every year, without fail, at least one guest chooses not to believe me. They never leave the same way they came—if they leave at all.

Jerry was one of them. Mid-twenties, passing through on his way to somewhere else; somewhere louder, faster, and far more exciting than our little town tucked between the folds of the hills.

When he arrived, I saw the kind of restlessness in his eyes that city folk carry like a second heartbeat. Phone in one hand, half-drunk coffee in the other, wearing the expression of someone who doesn't expect much from a place like this.

I checked him in, handed him the brass key, then led him to the back deck. The sun was sinking behind the ridgeline, spilling gold over the garden and painting the woods in long, shadowed stripes. The air smelled of damp earth and honeysuckle.

He leaned against the railing, gaze caught by the line of iron candle lanterns. They stood like sentries along the porch's edge and hung from the fascia board, their blackened glass catching the dying light.

His question came the way it always does: "What's with all the lanterns? You collect antiques or something?"

I smiled faintly and gave him the same answer I'd given a hundred times before—every word true, though most folks don't think so.

"During the day, this is a safe, quiet town. Main Street's got good shops, the hiking trails through the hills are worth the trip, and the café down the way makes the best blackberry pie you'll ever have. And there's a Civil War-era cemetery just at the end of that path there." I pointed toward the darkening trees.

He tilted his head, phone in hand. "You a history buff?"

"Not exactly," I said. "I brought you out here to warn you. After dark—do not leave this porch without at least one of these lanterns. Two would be better. And make sure they're lit. Always."

His mouth curved in that half-smirk I'd seen before, he continued to scroll absently on his phone as I spoke, the blue glow painting his face. The same expression I'd seen on every disbeliever before—the mix of amusement and dismissal, as if my words were nothing but a campfire tale. "Why not?"

"Because that cemetery holds more than just old bones. Most of the graves are marked—people laid to rest with names, prayers, and someone to remember them. But scattered between them are others—unmarked, forgotten. The ones who never had anyone to send them off with love.

Those souls never moved on. They wander in the mist, empty and lost. At night, they search. And if you cross their path without a lantern, they'll cling to you—thinking you're their way back. They don't mean harm, but they'll drag you with them all the same."

I let the silence stretch before adding, "Worse still is the creature that holds them in the mist. No one knows what it is. It comes every night with the fog, and the only thing that keeps it at bay are these lanterns."

I lifted one, its glass still warm from earlier use. "Vanilla and sage, laced with white magic enchantments," I said. "My wife makes them by hand. Only these candles work—ordinary candles, flashlights, phone lights, anything electric… useless. It has to be this exact blend of herbs and white magic, burning in candlelight."

"You telling me your wife's a witch?" He chuckled, shaking his head.

"She is what you would call a curandera, a white witch, a healer who uses herbal remedies and spiritual practices for protection, healing and good." I leaned closer, lowering my voice. "Her people have lived on this land for more than five hundred years—long before there was a town, before the church bell tolled over the valley, before the cemetery on the ridge was seeded with the bones of settlers. They came when the hills were wild and untamed, when the rivers still carried stories from the mountains and every grove of trees had its own spirit watching. They knew the language of herbs, the rhythms of the moon, the secrets hidden in the crackle of a fire, and the names of all the spirits both kind and cruel.

"Travelers came from far away, some limping with sickness, others carrying sorrow heavier than any wound. They sought out her people for their healing—poultices that drew fever away like smoke from coals, charms that turned aside misfortune, potions brewed under a waxing moon to bring luck or fertility. Back then, healing was done by the light of day, hands steady, voices calm. But at night, their work was different. When the veil between worlds thinned, they kept the land free of restless souls. With smoke and candle flame, with prayers and certain words spoken only in the old tongue, they guided the newly dead to the other side, making sure no spirit lingered long enough to sour into something darker.

"But sometime in the late 1700s, something stirred in the hollow beyond the ridge. No one knows if it was born from the land itself or if it drifted here from some older, blacker place. The first to see it gave it a name in fear—the Hollow Hunger. Some whispered it was grief made flesh, the first widow's wail given a body, or perhaps a shadow of the earth itself, hungry for warmth. Whatever its birth, it had no face, only a presence. All I know is this: it always comes back. It is drawn to breath and heartbeat the way a wolf is drawn to blood.

"It is older than memory, older than the stones buried under moss. A shadow that walked in fog before there was fog. At first it fed on those who died alone—the forgotten, the unmarked graves, the lost ones whose names slipped from memory. But it was never satisfied. Once it stripped them of what little they had left, it twisted their grief and confusion into mist, weaving a fog that never lifts. That fog became its hunting ground. In it, souls wander forever, lost in half-remembered lives, while the Hunger gorges itself on any living fool who dares to step inside.

"My wife's family fought it for generations. They learned what little could hold it back: the bitter smoke of juniper, salt in the doorways, candles kept burning through the night, and words in the old language that must never be spoken wrong. They tried again and again to destroy it—binding spells, fire, even blood sacrifice—but the Hollow Hunger only retreated, patient as the grave. By the time we inherited this place, it already owned the night.

"So, we do the only thing left: we keep the lanterns lit. Always burning. Always ready. They are not decoration, not mere tradition, but a line of fire between us and the fog.

As long as the lights hold, the Hunger keeps its distance. But should they falter, even for a breath, the mist will come rolling back, and with it the thing that waits inside. That's why the candles are here. That's why the lamps never go dark."

"That's quite a tale." He gave a short laugh. "You tell this to everyone?"

"Only the ones I want to see again," I said.

He grinned, thinking I was joking. I knew then how the night would end.

I woke to the scream.

It tore through the stillness like glass breaking in my chest. The clock read 2:39 a.m.

I ran to the back door, my wife at my heels. As I stepped onto the porch, I knew she would start her work—holding the mist back just enough for me to search for that foolish young man.

Taking a lantern in each hand, their flames flaring as if they knew where I was headed, I stepped forward. The air was cold enough to sting my lungs. A wall of mist pressed just beyond the rail, curling and shifting like something alive. The ring of lanterns along the porch guttered faintly, holding it at bay.

Beyond them, the night was soundless. Not even the crickets dared sing. Somewhere deep in the fog, I thought I heard the faintest weeping, but it vanished almost like vapor.

Cautiously, I stepped into the fog. The lanterns made two trembling, overlapping circles of light around me, but beyond them, shadows pressed close. The air was bitter and stale, smelling of wet stone and something older—like the inside of a tomb.

Now and then, the fog throbbed faintly, like it was

breathing. Once, I could swear I heard footsteps matching mine. When I stopped, so did they, but I knew I couldn't worry about that now. I needed to continue my search.

Step by step, the cemetery emerged from the haze, stones jutting like crooked teeth. Moss clung to angels with broken wings. Names swam in and out of sight as the fog slid between graves.

"Jerry!" I called. My voice felt muffled, swallowed by the mist.

No answer.

I searched for over an hour—down each narrow row, past cracked statues and tilted crosses—listening for footsteps, breath, or the faintest cry. Once, I thought I saw movement—a pale shape gliding just at the edge of the lantern light—but when I turned toward it, the mist closed in like a curtain.

No footprints. No torn cloth. No nothing.

When I returned to the porch, the mist lingered at the steps, as though watching. I lit two more lanterns and placed them at the base of the stairs, their flames swaying in unison.

⁂

Stepping inside, I shook my head at my wife, and she nodded in understanding as I picked up the phone. "Hello, Maybel. Get me Sheriff Taylor."

A click, then his voice—thick with sleep but not surprise. "Sheriff Taylor here."

"It's happened again," I said. "Name's Jerry Rosencrans. I looked for him, but he's gone. Lost now."

A long slow breath whistled on the other end. "Didn't you warn him?"

"Yes, sir," I said, watching my wife continue to chant for his lost soul. "I told him to take a lantern."

Another pause. "In the morning, gather his things and

bring them to me."

"Will do."

I disconnected, then my gaze drifted to the kitchen window, and I froze.

On the porch railing, just beyond the last lit lantern, was a handprint. Damp. Too large to be mine.

The mist shifted, parting just enough to show a pale, blurred face—Jerry's face, eyes wide, mouth moving as if to speak.

I bolted out the door, shoving my arm into the mist, praying he'd grasp it. For a breathless second, cold fingers latched onto me—clammy, desperate.

I caught one last, agonized glimpse of Jerry's face before the fog pulled him back. Behind him, shadow-thin shapes gathered—more than one—heads turning toward me, their forms wrong in ways my mind refused to understand.

They surged, yanking me forward. My boots slid over the wet boards. Cold seeped into my bones. The smell of earth and rot filled my lungs.

I grabbed for the railing, but I was losing ground.

My wife came running, lantern in hand, chanting in the ancient tongue of her ancestors. The flame flared, spilling gold through the fog. The shapes recoiled, their grip loosening just enough for me to wrench free.

The mist shuddered, then slowly withdrew to the edge of the lantern light.

I stood shaking, my wrist throbbing where they had touched me. A pale, ghostly claw print burned into my skin—cold to the touch. My wife did all she could, but even with her magic, we know it will never fade.

Morning came cold and pale. The lanterns still burned on the porch, their wax hardened, their scent faintly lingering in the air. The mist had retreated, leaving the garden damp and quiet.

I stepped off the deck, hoping against hope for some sign of him. That's when I saw it: a single, small object lying in the grass by the first lantern step.

Jerry's phone. Screen cracked, streaked with mud… and still warm. My heart thumped. A faint smear of a claw mark—too large for my hand, not human—streaked the glass.

I turned toward the cemetery path. The morning mist had lifted, yet somewhere deep in the trees, I thought I heard it: a faint whisper, high and trembling, calling my name.

"Lantern…"

I froze. The word hung in the air, carried on the wind. I didn't answer.

From the corner of my eye, movement—pale, almost translucent—just beyond the garden. Jerry. Or something wearing his shape. Watching. Waiting. His lips moved soundlessly, shaping words I couldn't hear. His eyes—too pale, too wide—never blinked.

The mist hadn't let him go. Not really. And it would be ready again, each night, for the next guest who didn't take a lantern.

The flames flickered as if warning me. I nodded, almost to myself. The rules were simple. Always the same.

Just then, the crunch of gravel. A car coming up the drive. I wondered… would they heed my warning?

About

Sleuths' Ink began in 1996 when a group of mystery writers decided they needed a forum for their specific genre. Since its inception, the group has hosted a variety of speakers, including forensic personnel, law enforcement, criminals, forensic specialists, mystery writers and more.

Sleuths' Ink Mystery Writers is a nonprofit organization. They meet the second Saturday of every month and feature guest speakers from writing experts, forensics specialists and more.

www.ingramcontent.com/pod-product-compliance
Lightning Source LLC
LaVergne TN
LVHW031925090826
845145LV00018B/2835

* 9 7 8 1 9 7 0 5 6 0 1 3 8 *